JONATHAN HARLEN

Circus Berzerkus

ALLEN&UNWIN

First published in 2002

Copyright © Jonathan Harlen 2002

Allen & Unwin
83 Alexander Street
Crows Nest NSW 2065
Phone: (61 2) 8425 0100
Fax: (61 2) 9906 2218
Email: info@allenandunwin.com
Web: www.allenandunwin.com

National Library of Australia
Cataloguing-in-Publication entry:

Harlen, Jonathan, 1963– .
  Circus Berzerkus.

  For children aged 9–12 years.
  ISBN 1 86508 770 X.

  1. Circus – Juvenile fiction. 2. Ghosts – Juvenile fiction.
  I. Title.

A823.3

Designed by Wayne Harris
Set in 12/18 pt Goudy by Midland Typesetters, Maryborough
Printed by McPherson's Printing Group, Maryborough

10 9 8 7 6 5 4 3 2

Contents

1 Bombs Away!

Allow me to introduce myself. My name is Rajah, and I'm a circus elephant. Or should I say I *was* a circus elephant, as I died not so very long ago, at the ripe old age of sixty, while I was sleeping peacefully in my cage.

When I was alive I was famous for performing on top of a red box. It was a pretty ordinary sort of red box, just big enough and strong enough for a fully-grown male African elephant to stand on, but it meant a lot to me. On a hot summer's night I would get up on that box in the middle of the ring, in front of five thousand screaming fans, and drive them wild.

One trick I did was especially famous. I would stand on my hind legs and twirl around in circles, trumpeting as loudly as I could. Audiences loved it.

They could never get enough. But twirling around in circles and trumpeting can get a bit boring after a while, so to keep things interesting, I would hop.

I would hop on two legs first, then on one leg. Blindfolded. I was the only blindfolded hopping elephant the world has ever seen, and my blindfolded hopping act was guaranteed to whip even the sleepiest crowd into a frenzy.

I worked with acrobats, too, and led the grand parade around the ring at the end of the show. But my routine on the red box was always the show-stopper. A picture of me standing on that box was used in all the circus publicity. It was also painted on the side of all our trucks and semi-trailers, just below the words, 'Gumbo Circus Royale'.

The Gumbo Circus Royale was owned by a family called the Gumbos and it's really them I wanted to tell you about. In particular, I want to tell you about their only son Marvin, who was my best friend when I was alive.

Marvin was born to the circus. He came from a long line of distinguished performers. His father, Colin Gumbo, was a great magician, famous for pulling live fire-breathing dragons out of his under-pants. His grandfather, Kevin Gumbo, had been a juggler and a world-class trapeze artist. His great-grandfather, Bevan Gumbo, had been a lion-tamer, while his great-great-grandfather, Irwin Gumbo – the founder of the show – had been a strongman.

Marvin's mother Olwyn was also a performer. She was a trapeze artist. She performed with a troupe of nine female acrobats called the Gumbo-ettes.

When you come from a family like that, there's pretty much only one way you can go. No one in the Gumbo household ever sat around saying things like 'How'd you like to be a fireman when you grow up, Marvin?' or 'Look at him pulling the tail off that lizard! I think he's going to be a vet!' When Marvin was only three years old, his mother set him up on my back, and I took him for his first elephant ride around the ring. From that moment on his one ambition in life was to follow in the footsteps of his famous forebears, and perform in the magnificent Gumbo Circus Royale.

Only one problem stood in the way of this ambition. Marvin didn't have an act. He was good at a lot of circus things, but not *spectacular* at anything. And at some things he was a complete no-hoper.

When he was ten years old, he tried to become a magician like his father. He practised pulling live fire-breathing dragons from his underpants, day and night, for hours at a time. In the end, after weeks of trying, the only thing he managed to pull from his own underpants was a small and rather smelly dead squid.

'A *squid*!' Colin Gumbo exclaimed in disgust. 'You pulled a *squid* from your underpants? That's ridiculous! Nobody's going to pay to see *that*!'

'There's no need to get upset, Colin,' Olwyn Gumbo said. 'He's only young. And anyway, what's wrong with a squid? I think squids are cute.'

'It's *dead*, that's what's wrong with it!' Colin Gumbo said. 'It's not even a *live* squid! It can't even *swim*! No Gumbo in history ever pulled a dead squid from their underpants! It's not part of the family tradition! Now get that horrible slimy thing out of my sight!'

Next Marvin tried to become an acrobat like his mother. He spent weeks practising the human pyramid with the Gumbo-ettes. Time after time he raced across the ring, leapt onto the springboard, soared through the air – and smashed into his mother and the other acrobats like a supersonic wrecking ball, sending them flying in all directions.

'Maybe you should take up a different hobby for a while,' Olwyn suggested kindly. 'Like train-spotting. Or collecting teaspoons.'

'Never!' Marvin replied. 'This is just a minor

setback! I've said I'm going to be a circus performer, and a circus performer is what I'm going to be!'

As it turned out, Marvin's wish came true sooner than we could have predicted. The way it happened was quite remarkable. In fact, it was so remarkably remarkable that you may find parts of it hard to believe.

But you can trust an elephant. Especially a dead one. Dead elephants never tell lies.

The day began like any other at the circus. It was mid-morning and a dress rehearsal was in full swing inside the Big Top. Marvin was on my back, as usual, and we were standing in a corner, waiting for the circus hands to bring in my red box.

Colin Gumbo was decked out in his ringmaster's uniform, complete with an enormous top-hat and a multi-coloured waistcoat. He was busy pulling live fire-breathing dragons out of his underpants.

Olwyn Gumbo and the Gumbo-ettes were practising their human pyramid, and doing triple backwards flips onto the backs of two other elephants, Daisy and Nellie.

The circus strongman, the Great Zambini, was juggling three Shetland ponies, a nanny goat, a Great Dane, and an echidna. (He usually juggled horses, but the horses were having a rest that morning.)

Dancing Dan the lion-tamer was off in a corner with his lions, Queenie, Princess, Empress and King. He was practising his famous 'Tonsil Tickler'. He hypnotised his lions by tap-dancing in front of them, then stuck his head so far down their throats that his nose tickled their tonsils.

On the high-dive platform, Knuckles the Clown and his troupe of six Madagascan monkeys were practising their comedy act. They were getting ready for their spectacular grand finale, when Knuckles dived head-first from the platform and fell forty metres into half a bucket of water.

Then there was Chubby Cupcakes. She was the circus Fat Lady. She weighed four hundred and fifty-nine kilos, or roughly the same as a small to medium-sized rhinoceros. She was so enormous that she had her own forklift to lift her in and out of her caravan. She was also a trapeze artist. She would hurtle back and forth across the ring on her trapeze, shouting 'Geronimo-o-o-o!' and 'Bombs away-y-y-y-y, ladies and gentlemen! Watch out belo-o-o-ow!', as the crowd screamed and ducked for cover.

It was a beautiful morning. The birds were shining brightly, and the sun was singing. But then, into this calm and pleasant scene came a mean, vicious gangster named Dave the Dirty Dog.

Dave the Dirty Dog was a small, weaselly-looking man who made his living by robbing and threatening people. He had heard there was a circus in town, and decided it would make easy pickings. So he cruised uninvited into the circus compound, driving a brand-new red Porsche.

He saw that everyone was inside the Big Top, so he drove his Porsche straight in through the open entrance, into the ring. He ran over the Great Zambini's echidna, squashing it flat. He bumped one of Olwyn Gumbo's elephants, causing six of the Gumbo-ettes to fall in a heap.

Immediately Colin Gumbo stormed across to ask him what the hell he was doing.

'What the hell are you doing?' Colin said. 'This is a restricted area! You can't come in here!'

Dave the Dirty Dog got out of the Porsche. He drew back his suit jacket to reveal a gun tucked into his belt.

'Shut up you flea-bitten old buzzard, and listen,' he snarled. 'My name's Dave the Dirty Dog, and I run this town. If you want to perform here you'll pay me five hundred dollars a day protection money, no questions asked. If you do that, I'll leave your circus alone. If you don't, you may find that some very unfortunate accidents start to happen.'

Colin Gumbo was a proud man, and a very brave one too. He wasn't scared of a small weaselly-looking gangster with a gun.

'You wouldn't be threatening me, would you?' he said. 'Because I don't like being threatened.'

'I'm just telling you the facts of life,' Dave the Dirty Dog said. 'Either you pay me the money, or somebody around here gets hurt. Which one's it gunna be?'

'Get out,' Colin Gumbo said, and pointed towards the door. 'Get in your car and go. I don't take orders from miserable little sewer-rats like you.'

Dave the Dirty Dog was thunderstruck. No one had ever talked to him like that before. He almost shot Colin Gumbo dead on the spot, but he knew better than to shoot his enemies in broad daylight, in front of witnesses.

'You'll regret this,' he hissed. 'Nobody says no to Dave the Dirty Dog. Nobody, you understand?'

He got back inside the Porsche and slammed the door. He was about to start the engine when I decided it was time to act.

I walked forward, stepped onto the bumper-bar, and began climbing up the bonnet onto the roof.

Then, when I got there, I stood on my hind legs and twirled around in a circle.

'Raj!' Marvin shouted from my shoulders. 'Raj, get down! This isn't your red box! It's a sports car! And there's a man inside it!'

No kidding, I thought. *Gee, I could have sworn it was my red box. If you ask me, it's just crying out to be stood on.*

I finished my twirls and began to hop. I hopped first on one leg, then the other. With each hop, the top of the car crumpled downwards with a loud crunching sound and a tinkling of glass.

Dave the Dirty Dog screamed in terror. He tried to start the car but the engine had just been stood on by a five-tonne circus elephant. It wouldn't move. As the roof came crashing down around him, he tumbled out the door and onto the ring.

'My car!' he howled. 'My beautiful Porsche! It's being pummelled into a pizza!'

He took out his gun and aimed it right between my eyes. I thought I was a goner for sure. Just then Knuckles the Clown gave a loud whistle. From high above, one of his monkeys leapt from the platform and snatched Dave's gun out of his hands. But Dave the Dirty Dog had *another* gun, in the pocket of his waistcoat. He pulled it out, ready to shoot me again.

This time it was Marvin who saved me. Suddenly, without any thought for his own safety, he leapt. He flew off my shoulders onto Dave the Dirty Dog's back, and tried to wrestle the gun away. Dave the Dirty Dog grabbed Marvin and lifted him up, ready to punch him as hard as he could.

Then the really remarkable thing happened. Chubby Cupcakes the Fat Lady dropped out of the sky. She swung down on her trapeze, then let go at exactly the right moment, so that her huge four-hundred-and-fifty-nine-kilo body crashed straight into Dave the Dirty Dog. Unfortunately she also crashed straight into Marvin, and sent both of them tumbling twenty metres across the ring.

When the sawdust settled, three people lay unconscious in a heap. Marvin was underneath Dave the Dirty Dog. Dave the Dirty Dog was underneath Chubby Cupcakes the Fat Lady. Chubby was rolling her head from side to side and moaning quietly.

'Quick, get the forklift!' Colin Gumbo shouted. 'We need to lift Chubby off! Marvin, are you all right? Say something!'

The forklift soon arrived, and the driver lifted Chubby off. Dave the Dirty Dog was still unconscious. Colin Gumbo tied him up, and put him in a corner, guarded by Dancing Dan's lions, until the police arrived.

As for Marvin, he was scraped carefully off the floor, and rushed to hospital in an ambulance.

2 A Legend Is Born

A team of doctors performed emergency surgery on Marvin all through the night. When morning came, they reported back to his parents.

'You've got a lot to be thankful for,' the head doctor told Colin and Olwyn Gumbo. 'Quite frankly, it's a miracle your son is still alive. For anyone to have a four-hundred-and-fifty-nine-kilo Fat Lady drop on them out of the sky, and live to tell the tale, is highly unusual. It's like having two grand pianos land on your head.'

'It's wonderful that he's still alive,' Colin Gumbo said. 'But now tell us the bad news. Is he squashed? Is he mangled? Is he crippled?'

'No, nothing like that,' the doctor said. 'Although it was touch-and-go there for a while. His kidney was up where his liver should have been. His lungs were down below his heart. His ribcage was sticking out his left shoulder, and his stomach was behind his right knee. But we managed to sort all that out. The only real damage was to his spine.'

'His spine!' Olwyn Gumbo gasped. 'Oh, my poor baby! Will he ever walk again?'

'Yes, I'm sure he will,' the head doctor said. 'No bones have been broken, and no nerves have been damaged, which is another miracle. But the spine itself has been completely flattened by the force of the impact. All the vertebrae have been pulled apart and stretched. He is now exactly now six and a half centimetres taller than he was before the accident, and his spine is still quite . . . elastic.'

'Elastic?' Olwyn Gumbo said. 'What d'you mean, elastic? Do you mean my son has been turned into a rubber band?'

'We don't know what it means yet,' the head doctor admitted. 'He's still too weak to move. But with a spine like that, who knows what he'll be capable of? It's not like any other spine we've ever seen.'

And so the first remarkable thing happened. Marvin survived being landed on by Chubby Cupcakes the Fat Lady. He returned home a month later to a hero's welcome.

Right at the very front of the crowd, waiting eagerly for their first glimpse of the returning hero, was a group of newspaper and television reporters. They hushed as Marvin stepped out of the car. We had all heard about his flattened spine, but at first glance nothing appeared different. Only if you looked closely could you see that Marvin wasn't the same.

He was taller and thinner. His arms and legs were loose and gangly. As he walked his body seemed to sway slightly, back and forth, like seaweed in a gentle ocean current.

Lightbulbs flashed. Cameras clicked and hummed. The reporters began calling out questions, one after the other.

'Marvin, are you better now?'

'Is it true you were ready to die to save your elephant?'

'What did it feel like to have the fattest woman in the world land on you? Did it hurt?'

'Yes, I am better now,' Marvin replied. 'And yes, I was ready to die to save my elephant. And as for how it felt to have Chubby land on top of me, let's just say that I know how the dinosaurs felt when they got hit by the giant meteor that wiped them out.'

'Marvin, we've all read the reports saying how

much your spine has been stretched,' one of the reporters said. 'What does this mean for you exactly? Does it mean you can do things that other people can't?'

Marvin shrugged modestly. 'A few things, yes,' he said.

'Like what?'

'Oh, nothing very important. Nothing worth writing about in your paper.'

'Can you tell us?' another reporter said. 'Or better still, can you give us a quick demonstration?'

Olwyn Gumbo stepped in front of her son. 'Thank you, ladies and gentlemen,' she said. 'I'm afraid Marvin's tired. He's only just been released from hospital. He's had a long day, and this probably isn't the best time for demonstrations.'

'I don't mind, Mum,' Marvin said. 'I'm happy to show what I can do. It's just a little trick I learned when I was recovering from my operation.'

The crowd watched expectantly. Marvin slowly got down on his knees, facing away from them. He leaned forward and put his head between his legs.

Then he began to stretch his elastic spine. He stretched it more and more, craning his neck and curving his back until his face, quite incredibly, appeared *on the other side of his legs*, facing backwards.

The crowd gasped. Marvin smiled. 'You ain't seen nothing yet, folks,' he said.

And with one final, superhuman stretch, he did the impossible. He puckered his lips, turned his head sideways, and kissed his own bottom.

'Look!' murmured the crowd. 'Look at *that*!'

'It's incredible!'

'It's miraculous!'

'I've never seen anything like it!'

'*The boy can kiss his own bum!*'

Just to show it was no fluke, Marvin turned his head the other way, and kissed the other side of his bottom. The crowd burst into rapturous applause.

'Bravo! Bravissimo!' the cries went up. 'Encore! Encore!'

'That's enough now, ladies and gentlemen,' Olwyn Gumbo said. 'Marvin really is tired. Thank you very much for coming, and I hope we'll see you at our circus again soon.'

That evening, Marvin and his parents had a long and serious talk. Colin Gumbo was beside himself with excitement. He'd been in the circus game a long time. He knew that Marvin's trick, simple though it seemed, was in fact incredibly difficult. It had long been the ultimate challenge, the Holy Grail of contortionists and India-Rubber-Men everywhere.

Throughout history, many people had tried to kiss their own bottoms. None had succeeded. Even the great masters had given up in despair. Some had broken their necks. Some had suffocated. Others had got to within centimetres – *millimetres* – of their target, only to fail and die of a broken heart.

'You have to understand, son,' Colin Gumbo said, 'that this new talent of yours is a gold mine. It's your ticket to fame and fortune. It's a trick that no one in history has ever been able to perform, and you've done it in front of television cameras and news photographers, so we have *proof* that you've done it. By tomorrow morning, those pictures of you kissing your own bottom will have gone all around the world.'

'But is it enough for an act?' Marvin asked. 'It's only one trick, after all. And not a very long trick either.'

'Is it enough for an *act?*' Colin Gumbo spluttered. 'My boy, haven't you been listening? Don't you realise what you've done? People have been trying for *centuries* to kiss their own bottoms! It's like climbing Mount Everest! It's like solving the mysteries of the pyramids! *Of course* it's enough for an act! It will be the most brilliant circus act the world has ever seen!'

16

3 The Warning

Colin Gumbo's prediction proved correct. The next morning, TV footage of Marvin's amazing achievement was beamed around the world. Every major daily newspaper from Hawaii to Helsinki carried a large colour photograph of Marvin on its front page, together with a headline announcing the story.

BOY KISSES OWN BOTTOM! the headlines screamed. *HISTORY MADE BY SON OF GREAT CIRCUSING FAMILY! A DREAM OF AGES HAS BEEN REALISED! A CENTURIES-LONG WAIT IS OVER! THE STUNNING ACHIEVEMENT OF MARVIN GUMBO BRINGS JOY TO A SUFFERING WORLD!*

'Well, I don't know about *that*,' Colin Gumbo

said at the breakfast table, as he sipped his tea and read the papers. 'That might be going a bit far.'

'Here's a headline from a French paper,' Olwyn Gumbo said. ' "GARCON S'EMBRASSE LE DERRIERE!" D'you think it means . . .?'

'I'm sure it does,' Colin Gumbo said. 'Here's the same thing in Italian, too. "RAGAZZO BACIO IL PROPRIO SEDERE!" '

'And here it is in German. And Japanese. And Indonesian.' Olwyn Gumbo thumbed through the stack of papers on the table, and sighed proudly. 'Just think. All over the world, right at this very moment, the entire population of planet Earth is talking about our son's bottom.'

'Yes, and the next thing is, they're going to want to see it,' Colin Gumbo said. 'They'll want it live and pimply, in the flesh. You wait and see, my dear. After this we'll have thousands of people wanting tickets to the circus. *Tens* of thousands. We're going to be run off our feet.'

Once again Colin Gumbo was right. That same day, ticket sales soared. By the end of the week, a month's worth of extra performances were booked out, and the frenzy showed no sign of slowing.

Two weeks later Marvin made his first appearance under the Big Top. It was a sensation. At the very end of the night, after all the other acts had finished, Colin Gumbo stepped up to the microphone to make an announcement.

'Ladies and gentlemen!' he boomed. 'The Gumbo Circus Royale is proud to present the act you've all been waiting for! The amazing child prodigy! The next wonder of the circusing world! Defying all laws of gravity and physics and biology to give you the body-twisting, back-to-front thrill of a lifetime, would you please welcome the boy with the elastic spine, the one and only . . . MARVIN GUMBO!!!!

The roar that followed nearly raised the roof. Marvin appeared in the spotlight at the entrance to the ring. He was barefoot, and dressed like a gymnast in white leotards and a white top. He waved to the wildly cheering crowd, then began walking out across the ring.

When he reached the middle he stopped and raised his hands. The crowd hushed.

Marvin got down on his knees, lowered his head between his thighs, and stretched his amazing elastic spine until his head appeared, facing out the back of his own legs.

He stopped.

He waited.

The crowd held its breath.

A small rotating stage burst out of the ground underneath Marvin. It lifted him ten metres into the air, and held him there, turning slowly.

Marvin tilted his head. He puckered his lips and stretched just that little bit further, further than anyone in history had ever stretched before.

Lips and buttock met in a perfectly executed kiss.

Lights blazed. Drums rolled. Trumpets blared. Streamers and confetti dropped from the ceiling. Olwyn Gumbo and her Gumbo-ettes came dancing into the ring and formed a circle around Marvin as the crowd erupted once again into deafening cheers.

It was a wonderful moment. Marvin's childhood dream had been realised. He was a star in The Gumbo Circus Royale.

We could never have guessed how quickly the dream would turn into a nightmare.

The rest of us were watching backstage, waiting for the farewell parade of the evening. I was at the front, preparing to lead the parade. Chubby Cupcakes was positioned just behind me on her forklift, and as the deafening cheers for Marvin rang out, she surprised us all by starting to cry.

'I'm so p-p-proud!' she sobbed to Knuckles the Clown. 'To think, if I hadn't c-c-crashed into him at a hundred k's an hour and sq-squashed him flat, none of this would have happened!'

'You should have crashed into him at *two* hundred k's an hour, and crippled the little beggar,' Dancing Dan growled. 'My agent warned me never to work with children. Look at him. He's getting louder cheers than any of us – and for what? What's so special about kissing your own bottom?'

'Can you do it?' Knuckles asked.

'I wouldn't want to do it,' Dancing Dan sneered. 'I wouldn't want to pick my nose with my toe either. Or poke out my eyeball with a stick. What *I* do takes class. It takes style. I wouldn't be seen dead pulling a cheap, worthless stunt like that.'

I could tell straight away that Dancing Dan was jealous. It wasn't hard to figure out why. Never, in all his years of performing, had he been upstaged like this. He believed *he* was the real star of the show, and until Marvin came along, he was.

Dancing Dan was a tall, handsome man with black hair and a swashbuckling smile. He had started out his career as a singer and dancer, working in musicals. Then, at the age of thirty, he'd discovered an amazing hidden talent.

He went on safari in Africa, but on the last day he got lost. For two weeks he trudged alone through the wilds of Botswana, with ferocious predators stalking him at every turn. Finally, almost dead from exhaustion, he was cornered at the edge of a cliff by a pride of starving lions, who closed in for the kill.

Dancing Dan did the only thing he could think of to save the situation. He burst into song.

A snappy rendition of 'When My Baby Smiles at Me I Go to Rio' hypnotised the lions into submission. A toe-tapping flamenco dance routine reduced them to putty in his hands. Not only did the lions not eat him, they formed a guard of honour to protect him, and went with him all the way back to civilisation.

When he returned, Dancing Dan gave up performing in musicals. He used his new-found talents to create the most fantastic lion-taming routine the world had ever seen, and became famous overnight.

Unfortunately, fame was not a good thing for Dancing Dan. It went straight to his head. He demanded twice as much money as the other performers, and twice as much time on stage. He also wanted his name to be twice as big in all the advertising.

He insisted that the Gumbos supply a dozen bottles of French champagne to his caravan after each show, and that they lay a red carpet to his front door.

The morning after Marvin's show-stopping appearance, watching from my cage, I saw Dancing Dan come out of his caravan onto the red carpet to pick up his daily newspaper. He looked as though he'd had no sleep. He was unshaven and unwashed. His pyjamas and dressing gown were a disgrace.

He was holding an empty bottle of French champagne in his hand.

Been on the turps all night, have you Dan? I thought. That's definitely not a good sign.

He picked up the newspaper and opened it. *BOY KISSES OWN BOTTOM AGAIN!* the headlines screamed. *MARVIN GUMBO DOES IT LIVE AND SWEATY! NEW ERA IN CIRCUS PERFORMING BRINGS MORE JOY TO SUFFERING WORLD!*

'What?' Dan exclaimed. 'There's nothing in here about me at all! Not a word! Not a single photo! This is too much! Something has GOT to be done!'

He flung the paper to the ground and set off, still in his pyjamas and dressing gown, towards Colin Gumbo's office caravan next to the Big Top. As soon as he'd gone past, I did something I hadn't done in a long time. I searched with the tip of my trunk under the straw in the corner of my cage, and found the spare key that Marvin had given me for emergencies. I unlocked my cage door and followed Dan as quickly as I could.

I snuck up to the window of Colin Gumbo's office caravan and peered inside. Dancing Dan was ranting and raving in front of Colin's desk, while Colin sat looking stunned.

'I refuse to share the ring with a stupid talentless child performing a cheap schoolboy prank!' Dancing Dan shouted. 'It's preposterous! There's no skill in what he does! There's no artistry, or refinement, or finesse! I want him out of the show by tonight or I quit, and that's my last word!'

'I'm sorry, Dan, but I can't do that,' Colin Gumbo replied calmly. 'Right now Marvin is our biggest star. The whole country is fighting to get tickets to see him. It's nothing personal – it's just showbiz. You're a professional, I'm sure you understand.'

'I *understand*,' said Dancing Dan through gritted teeth, 'that my own hard-earned reputation is being ruined by a wretched little twerp who slobbers over his own bum! I demand that you get rid of him! It's him or me!'

'Fine,' Colin Gumbo said. 'It's you. You're fired.'

'*What!*' Dancing Dan howled. 'You can't do that! This circus is nothing without me! I made you Gumbos everything you are today!'

'You're a top-class performer and I pay you well for it,' Colin Gumbo replied. 'But you don't tell me who gets to perform in my own circus. Marvin stays, and he continues to get top billing, and if you don't like it you can leave, right now. It's as simple as that.'

Dancing Dan fell silent. Angry as he was, he could see that Colin Gumbo wasn't going to back down. In the past, when Dan had demanded twice as much pay as everyone else, and twice as much time in the ring, and a dozen bottles of champagne in his dressing room every night, Colin Gumbo had given in without much of a fight. But not this time.

'All right,' Dancing Dan said finally. 'Let the little brat do whatever he likes. But I'm warning you, Gumbo, you haven't heard the last of this. It's a tough world out there. You'd better hope your precious little son has got what it takes, otherwise he'll be chewed up and spat out in the gutter before you can say "Gumbo Circus Royale".'

4 Rajah's Return

A few days later, I spotted Dancing Dan lurking around the lion's cages. It was evening, not long after feeding time, and still a couple of hours before the show was due to begin.

My own cage was next to Queenie's, so I got a very good view of what happened next. Dancing Dan walked right up to Queenie and began scratching her under the chin.

'It's time to get serious about this, Queenie,' he said. 'It's time to show young Master Gumbo we mean business. We can't have him being the biggest star instead of me, can we? That's out of the question. It's time to tragically end Marvin Gumbo's short but brilliant circus career.'

I pricked up my ears. Elephants have extremely

sensitive hearing, but I wasn't as young as I used to be, and my trusty old lugflaps weren't exactly razor-sharp.

'The real question is, can it be made to look like an accident?' Dan said. 'I wouldn't want you to *kill* him. Just bite off a leg or an arm, so he can never perform again. The trouble is, you might get a taste for it, mightn't you? You might finish the entrée and decide you want the main course as well.'

Queenie was clearly enjoying the neck scratch, but I don't think she understood much of what Dan was saying. Lions are pretty dumb, if you must know. Any creature that has to run down a gazelle or an antelope just to get a bite to eat is obviously missing a few spoons from the top drawer.

I understood, though. I snorted and stamped my feet in rage – and heard the wooden floor beneath me give a loud creak.

Dan turned his head. 'What do you want, you mangy old fossil?' he snapped.

I flapped my ears and trumpeted. Dan came over and stood with his arms folded, just out of my reach.

'I've never liked you, wrinkle-features,' he said. 'In fact, of all the sorry creatures in this miserable dump, you're the one I hate the most. One day, when I'm so famous I can buy this circus and ruin the

Gumbos completely, I'm going to have you shot. Your carcass should be enough to keep a dog-food factory going for a week.'

Dan didn't know about the spare key I kept under the straw in my cage. If he had, he might have been a touch more polite.

'I'm not sure, though, Queenie,' Dan said, returning once again to the lions' cage. 'It's risky. There's always the chance they'll blame it on me, and I'll get thrown in prison. Maybe there's another option . . . something not so obvious, eh? And I'm sure you'd prefer not to be shot for attacking Marvin, wouldn't you, my girl?'

Shortly after that, he left. The circus started as usual at seven o'clock and I gave the worst perform-ance I'd ever given in my life. I was so upset that I couldn't do anything right. I twirled the wrong way. I lost my balance when I went up on two legs. As for my famous blindfolded hop, it was more like a blind-folded trip-and-fall-flat-on-my-backside. I couldn't wait to get back to my cage.

I stayed awake all that night, thinking about what Dan had said. Some time in the wee hours of the morning, I took a solemn oath. I vowed to do whatever I had to do, including give up my life, to protect my best friend Marvin from Dancing Dan.

This oath was to change a lot of things, in ways I never expected. But before I had the chance to act on it, something else happened.

This was an event so terrible, so utterly disastrous, that it sent stockmarkets tumbling all over the world, and plunged the whole of civilisation into chaos.

I died.

All right, it wasn't *that* terrible. It didn't *really* send stockmarkets tumbling, and most of civilisation didn't give a hoot. But it was still pretty bad for me.

One moment there I was, snoozing away happily after polishing off a late night snack of five dozen donuts, the next – *wham*! I was history. I'd kicked the bucket. I'd gone belly-up in the bowl. I'd dropped off the twig, cashed in my chips, unplugged the respirator, snuffed out the candle, and carked it.

I remember the moment of my death very clearly. All at once my body simply seized up and stopped working. My mind, however, went on exactly as before. Not only that, but it began floating, drifting free.

Invisible, lighter than air, I floated up to the top of my cage and hovered there, looking down on the scene below.

I knew straight away that I was going to become a ghost.

Now that it's all over, and I've left the mortal world behind forever, I can explain these things. Some creatures who die become ghosts, and some don't. Not many do, as a matter of fact, because in order to become a ghost you need to take an Oath of Protection, or an Oath of Revenge, some time in the last week before you die, and not many creatures do that.

Taking an Oath of Protection, as I did, allows your spirit to remain behind in the mortal world. It also means you can appear in solid form whenever you want to – but not forever. Each ghost only stays here for as long as it needs to fulfil its oath. Then it goes home.

The same goes for taking an Oath of Revenge. That also allows your spirit to remain in the mortal world for as long as it's needed. You'll hear more about that later.

Anyway, where was I? Oh yes. Invisible and weightless, floating around the top of my cage like a cloud with an outboard motor. I could move very fast, and go anywhere I wanted. I could also make myself visible and invisible as often as I liked. That first night, however, I only appeared in solid form once, to see if I could polish off the last of my donuts. I couldn't, though. I could pick the donuts up with my trunk, and put them in my mouth, but they tasted like nothing at all.

The day after I became a ghost, I had the honour of attending my own funeral. This was a very modest and tasteful affair, held at Stadium Australia, with around twenty thousand mourners. The Gumbos didn't spend nearly enough money on it, in my opinion, but there were still some nice touches.

They hired a massed church choir to sing hymns. They hired a regiment from the Army to fire a twenty-one-gun salute. They also hired a squadron of FA-18 Hornets from the Air Force to write WE LOVE YOU RAJAH in letters a kilometre high across the sky.

Throughout the service they played videos of me on the giant screen. They piled a thousand red roses under the goalposts. And for the soul-stirring grand finale the great Slim Dusty performed a beautiful and moving ballad he'd written specially for the occasion: 'You Are the Elephant of My Dreams'.

Rajah, oh Rajah, with you none compare
No lion or tiger, no monkey or bear
You stood on your red box and trumpeted loud
Deafening every last kid in the crowd
Your droppings were larger than Pizza Supremes
You are the elephant of my dreams.

Ah, yes. A modest and tasteful affair. Low-key from start to finish. Just the sort of quiet, dignified send-off I'd always wanted.

I was worried about Marvin, though. I'd been his best friend for years, and my death left him broken-hearted. At the end of the service, when two large cranes lowered my coffin into the enormous pit that had been dug at the half-way line, he cried and cried.

Worse still, he couldn't perform. He couldn't go back into the ring. I was deeply touched that he missed me so much, but the circus soon began to suffer. Marvin was the main attraction, and people didn't want to buy tickets if he was no longer there.

Colin and Olwyn Gumbo were desperate. One afternoon they tried to change Marvin's mind by telling him a story about his grandfather, Kevin Gumbo.

'You should try and remember what Grandad Kevin said to us on the day he died,' Olwyn Gumbo said. 'Grandad Kevin was ill in bed, and your father and I sat by him all that afternoon, holding his hand. Then, at seven o'clock on the dot, Grandad Kevin opened his eyes. He looked at us with a trembling smile, and whispered, "What are you two doing still here? It's showtime!"'

'Those were his last words to us, ever,' Colin

Gumbo added. 'When we'd finished performing and came back to the caravan, he was dead.'

'What!' Marvin exclaimed. 'You mean you weren't there with Grandad Kevin when he died? That's terrible!'

'We were only doing what he wanted, Marvin,' Colin Gumbo said. 'Your grandfather never missed a performance in his life. Not even when a freak cyclone picked up the Big Top and blew it into the middle of the Gibson Desert.'

'And my grandfather,' Marvin muttered, 'was obviously a complete nut.'

'No, he just didn't want to let his audience down,' Olwyn Gumbo said. 'And neither do we. That's why we want you to start performing again.'

Marvin thought this over. He shook his head. 'I'm sorry,' he said. 'I know it means a lot to you. But when someone you love dies, to me that's more important than any audience, or any show.'

Only one person was happy after my death, and that was Dancing Dan. With me no longer around to protect Marvin, he felt free to tease the poor boy as often as he liked.

'Hey, pipsqueak! Why the long face?' he would call out, as Marvin walked past his caravan. 'You look like someone whose elephant just died!'

If he spotted Marvin sitting alone inside my cage, he would call out, 'Marvin! You don't want to kiss your bottom today? Is it too smelly for you?'

In the past, Dan's teasing had never bothered Marvin. But since my death he wasn't the same. All the stuffing had been knocked out of him. And, just like a roast chook, the stuffing inside Marvin was the best part.

Something had to be done.

I waited patiently for the right time and place. This came one chilly autumn night ten weeks after I'd died, when Marvin climbed into my empty cage and sat staring at an old photo of me that he'd hung on the wall.

'What's wrong with me, Raj?' he said to the empty cage. 'I should be over your death by now but every time I think about going back into the ring, I dry up inside. I can't do it.'

In the blink of an elephant's eyelash, I materialised on the outside of the cage. I appeared in my normal form, and made myself look as solid as I could, so I looked as much like a real elephant as possible. I still had an eerie white glow around the edges. That couldn't be helped. But, if I say so myself, the overall effect wasn't too bad.

Marvin was so astonished that he leapt to his feet

and grabbed hold of the bars of the cage, all in a single movement.

'Rajah?' he whispered, wide-eyed. 'Raj, is that you?'

I raised my trunk and tapped on the door of the cage. Marvin backed away.

'Raj, you're dead!' he said hoarsely. 'You're buried five metres under the half-way line at Stadium Australia! This can't be you!'

I tapped on the door again, and flapped my ears.

'You want to take me for a ride?' Marvin said. 'But you can't! You can't do that, Raj! You're not real!'

I bumped my forehead against the side of the cage and pushed it, so that the wagon underneath lifted up on two wheels.

'Yeow!' Marvin exclaimed. 'All right, all right! You *can* take me for a ride! But I'm sorry, I don't understand what's going on.'

I set the cage down again. Marvin came down the ramp to stand beside me. He reached up to touch my shoulder. I raised my trunk and nuzzled at the back of his neck.

'I can feel you,' he mumbled. 'You're not even cold. Raj, is it really you?'

No, I wanted to say, *it's Skippy the kangaroo in an elephant suit*. But I didn't. I patiently tapped on the cage door once again.

'Oh yeah, the ride.' Marvin laughed nervously. 'Sure, why not? Everyone around here thinks I've lost the plot anyway. Wait till I tell them I went for a ride on a ghost elephant. Then they'll *really* think I'm crazy.'

I backed away, stamping my feet and snorting.

'You don't want me to tell them?' Marvin said. 'Fine. That's okay, Raj. I promise I won't tell a soul.'

That was a big relief. If Marvin told other people what he'd seen, they would tell more people, and those people would tell people, and pretty soon the circus would have a reputation for being haunted. I didn't think that would do it any good at all.

A minute later Marvin was up on my back, perched comfortably between my shoulders. It was wonderful to have him up there again. It was the best feeling I'd had in my entire death.

'This is amazing,' Marvin said. 'I never thought ghosts could do this. I guess the technology must be getting better, eh, old boy?'

I began walking towards the Big Top. All around us, the caravans and animal cages were dark and quiet. The only sound was of two monkeys chattering, and one or two horses neighing gently.

I took Marvin in through the rear entrance of the Big Top, past the backstage area and into the ring. I walked right out into the centre, to the exact spot where Marvin's rotating stage was buried under the sawdust. He hadn't been near that spot since the day I died.

I knew that coming back now would be hard. I knelt down to allow him to get off me, then waited.

Marvin stood staring out through the half-darkness at the rows and rows of empty seats. 'You want me to perform again,' he said finally. 'That's why you've brought me here, isn't it, Raj?'

I waited longer. Outside the tent, the wind sounded like the faint echo of cheers.

'I probably *could* perform again,' Marvin admitted. 'Now that I know you're here. If I perform you'll watch me, won't you, Raj?'

I flapped my ears.

'Every time? Even the Saturday matinees?'

I flapped my ears and raised my trunk.

'All right, I'll do it,' Marvin said. 'It'll be just like before. Except from now on, every show that I do, I'm going to dedicate to you.'

He turned once more to face the empty stands. 'Ladies and gentlemen!' he said. 'Boys and girls! This performance is in loving memory of Rajah, Prince of Pachyderms! May his soul rest in peace!'

He turned back to me and grinned. 'How does that sound?'

5 The Autograph

Just as he'd promised, Marvin returned to the ring the very next week. Before he began his act he took the microphone from his father and made a short announcement.

'Ladies and gentlemen, boys and girls, this performance is in loving memory of Rajah, Prince of Pachyderms,' he said. 'May his soul rest in peace. Thank you.'

His performance that night was exceptional. It was far better than the ones he'd given before I died. You might think there wasn't much to improve on, when all he did was stick his head between his legs and kiss his own bottom. But there was.

Now, when he kissed his own bottom, he did it with *soul*.

'Last night at the Gumbo Circus Royale, Marvin Gumbo moved me to tears,' one reviewer wrote. 'He stirred me to the very depths of my being. When his lips pressed passionately yet delicately against his own buttock, I almost fainted. There was more poetry and artistry in that one kiss than in all the Hollywood screen kisses combined.'

The following morning a newspaper containing this review landed with a thump on Dancing Dan's doorstep. He came out of his caravan to read it.

Since Marvin's return to the ring, Dan had gone downhill fast. He was staying up later than ever. He was drinking more and more champagne, leaving his empties on the table and on the floor. His dishes were unwashed. His clothes were heaped over the furniture. All he could think about was Marvin, and how Marvin had once again taken over from him as the circus's biggest star.

Dan turned to the review page to see a full-colour picture of Marvin, under the headline: *A KISS OF PURE BRILLIANCE AT THE GUMBO CIRCUS ROYALE*.

'What's wrong with these fools?' he muttered. 'How can they ignore me like this?'

Then he read the review that I've just quoted, and I'm afraid he lost his temper completely.

'Poetry?' he cried. 'Artistry? Stirred me to the very depths of my being? What a great stinking pile of steaming horse manure!'

He kicked out at a dozen empty champagne bottles stacked up on the doorstep. One of them hit the side of the caravan and smashed into a thousand pieces.

'I'll get you, Marvin Gumbo!' he shouted. 'Don't think the battle's over! It hasn't even started yet! I'll make you wish you'd never been born!'

Dan was teetering right on the brink of madness. And the very next night, something happened that pushed him right over the edge.

It happened after the show. Dan was just leaving the Big Top, on his way back to his caravan. I was hovering invisibly nearby, keeping watch in case he tried to hurt Marvin.

Suddenly a beautiful young woman came running towards us from the carpark. She was about twenty years old, and tall, with long brown hair.

'Excuse me,' she said breathlessly, 'You're Dancing Dan the lion-tamer, aren't you? Could you please help me?'

Dancing Dan never said no to a beautiful woman. He smiled his best lady-killer smile.

'Of course I can help you,' he said. 'It would be

an honour and a privilege. How may I be of assistance?'

'I'm looking for Marvin Gumbo,' the young woman said. 'I really need to get his autograph. Do you know where he is?'

Dancing Dan's smile froze. He clenched his fists.

'You're looking for Marvin,' he said through gritted teeth. 'How nice.'

'I'd give *anything* to get his autograph tonight,' the young woman sighed. 'It's the most important thing in the world to me right now. Do you know if he's still inside the Big Top?'

'Oh no,' Dan said, although he knew very well that Marvin *was* still inside the Big Top. 'It's way past his bedtime. He'll be curled up asleep with his teddy bear by now. Probably sucking his thumb. But there's no need to worry, my dear. This is your lucky night. I will give you *my* autograph instead!'

Dan reached out to take the young woman's pen and paper, but she stepped back, blushing.

'Thanks anyway,' she said. 'But it's really Marvin Gumbo's autograph that I want.'

This was too much for Dan. His face went purple, and his eyelid twitched.

'Perhaps you don't know who I am,' he snarled. 'I am Dancing Dan the lion-tamer, the most celebrated circus performer in history. I am *much* more famous than Marvin Gumbo.'

'Yes, I know who you are,' the girl said. 'And I enjoyed your show very much. But you see, I've got to get Marvin's autograph. I've just got to! I made a promise to someone, and—'

'Forget Marvin Gumbo!' Dan shouted. 'His autograph is worthless! He's a pathetic little twelve-year-old nobody who pulls dead squid from his underpants! Oh, I know he can kiss his own bottom these days. But so what? You call that entertainment? I, Dancing Dan, can make the King of the Beasts jump backwards through a flaming hoop! Women all over the world fight over me! They pay thousands of dollars for my autograph! What's wrong with you?'

By now the poor young woman was thoroughly baffled. All she wanted was to get Marvin's autograph for her ten-year-old little sister, who was very ill in hospital. But for some reason Dancing Dan was behaving like a complete prawn.

'I need to see Marvin,' she said firmly. 'I'll stay here and wait for him, if you don't mind.'

At that moment, Marvin emerged from the Big Top with his parents. The young woman gave a gasp of delight and ran straight up to him.

'Marvin!' she called out. 'Please, please can I have your autograph? I've been waiting hours!'

Dan watched, seething with rage, as Marvin took the pen and signed the autograph. When he'd finished, the young woman was so delighted that she threw her arms around Marvin and gave him a big wet kiss, right on the chompers. Then she gave him another big wet kiss, just for good measure.

'Thank you!' she gushed. 'Thank you so much! You've made one of your biggest fans very happy!'

After Marvin had left, I stayed behind to keep an eye on Dancing Dan. To say he was in shock would be an understatement. The man was a complete wreck. To see such a beautiful young woman hug and kiss Marvin instead of him was the last straw.

Dan wasn't just jealous any more. He was *insanely* jealous, and out for murderous revenge.

6 Desperate Measures

As soon as Dan had recovered, he went straight back to his caravan. He stomped around inside for a while, then came out with a small brown paper bag and a pair of scissors. Clutching these, he hurried across the compound to the caravan of his friend the Great Zambini, and pounded on the door.

The Great Zambini answered in his dressing gown, looking very bleary-eyed.

'Get your clothes on, you big oaf,' Dancing Dan said. 'You're coming with me.'

Although the Great Zambini was officially listed as the strongest man in the world – and the only man alive who could juggle horses – he was actually a gentle soul. He looked exactly like a strongman should look, with a huge bald head, a magnificent black handlebar moustache, and the muscles of a well-developed gorilla.

His costume was a pair of yellow tights and a yellow singlet with a red lightning flash on the front. This costume looked ridiculous, but nobody ever said that to the Great Zambini, because a man that big, with the muscles of a well-developed gorilla, can wear whatever he likes.

The Great Zambini also glowed in the dark. The veins and arteries just beneath the skin glowed especially brightly. At night these veins and arteries shone a bright neon blue, all over his body, and the Great Zambini lit up like a Christmas tree.

He glowed this way because he ate so many steroids. He ate steroids sprinkled on pasta for every meal.

For breakfast he ate fettucine carbonara sprinkled with steroids. For lunch he ate tortellini funghi sprinkled with steroids, washed down with two cups of Japanese herbal steroid tea. For dinner he had the same as he had for breakfast, and for supper he ate *steroids* sprinkled with steroids, followed by a large bowl of steroids and icecream for dessert.

He was glowing especially brightly when he joined Dancing Dan outside his caravan. A swarm of moths swooped down and fluttered all around him.

'Hey boss,' he said cheerfully, in his thick Italian

accent. 'Where we go tonight, huh?'

'To the lions' cages,' Dan said, as he swatted moths away angrily.

The Great Zambini frowned in puzzlement. 'Why we go to lions' cages?' he asked.

'Because that's where the lions are,' Dan said.

'Ah, *si, si*.' The Great Zambini nodded. 'That ees where the lions are. *Si*.'

They set off together across the grass. A short time later, Zambini said, 'But why we go to lions?'

'To cut off some lion's whiskers and put them in this paper bag.'

'Ah, *si, si*.' The Great Zambini nodded again. 'To cut lion's wheeskors and put een bag. Naturally.'

The two of them continued walking.

'But why—'

'Shhh!' Dan said. 'We're getting close now. We don't want any of the animals to wake up.'

Dan stopped next to Queenie's cage. He checked that Queenie was asleep, then took a large black key from his pocket, and unlocked the door.

'Come in,' he whispered to Zambini. 'She won't hurt you. Even if she wakes up, I'll hypnotise her. You hold the bag for me, okay?'

He handed the brown paper bag to Zambini. Then he held up the scissors to the moonlight, and grinned in delight.

'Now we'll show the little fancypants who's boss, won't we, Queenie?' he muttered, as if forgetting for a moment that Zambini was there. 'This'll fix him. This'll knock him off his perch. He won't feel like slobbering over his own bum after *this*, will he?'

'Why you need wheeskors?' Zambini asked stubbornly. 'Why you cut wheeskors and put in bag?'

'Shhhhh.' Dancing Dan signalled for him to be quiet. 'Don't ask too many questions. You'll strain yourself.'

Holding the scissors in front of him, Dancing Dan knelt down on the straw, as close as he dared to Queenie's fearsome jaws. He cupped his left hand underneath one of her long, thick whiskers, and with his right hand got ready to cut.

'Easy does it now,' he said. 'I need to cut it nice and close, right next to the skin—'

Without warning, Zambini grabbed Dancing Dan by the collar, and yanked him hard to his feet.

'I ask you one more time,' he said. 'Why you cut lion's wheeskors?'

'Are you crazy?' Dan hissed. 'You nearly woke Queenie! Let me go, you blithering idiot!'

'First you tell me why you cut lion's wheeskors,' Zambini said. 'Then I let you go.'

'All right, all right!' Dan looked furious, but he knew better than to argue with a man who could juggle horses. 'It's an old African witch-doctor's trick that I learned when I was on safari. You cut the lion's whiskers into tiny pieces, then sprinkle the chopped-up bits in someone's food. In this case, Marvin's food. Now will you please let me go?'

Listening from outside the cage, I froze. Being an African elephant, I knew all about the deadly lion's-whiskers-in-the-food trick. Witch-doctors had used it on their enemies for centuries. Zambini, however, still had no idea what Dan was talking about.

'You spreenkle wheeskors een food?' he said.

'Yes.'

'Why? What they do? They make food taste bad?'

'No, that's the whole point. You can't taste them. They prick tiny holes in the lining of the stomach.'

Zambini's frown deepened. 'You mean . . . Marveen he get hurt?'

'Well, no . . . I mean . . . not much,' Dan said, seeing the look of horror beginning to dawn on Zambini's face. 'Hardly at all, really. Just a mild stomache ache, so that he's too sick to perform.'

'I no want Marveen get hurt,' Zambini said. 'He jost a leetle keed.'

'You won't hurt him, I promise,' Dan said.

'I no hurt heem? Never?'

'Never.'

No, but you will, Dan, you murderous scheming monster, I thought. Those whiskers didn't only cause a mild stomach ache. They caused the victim to die in horrible agony. What's more, all the bits of whisker dissolved in the victim's stomach afterwards, so they couldn't be traced. Whoever put them in the food in the first place would get off scot-free.

'So you hold the bag,' Dan said to Zambini, 'and I'll chop up the whiskers and put them in. Then we can go home.'

Zambini didn't look convinced, but he nodded. 'Hokay.'

Dan knelt down a second time and prepared to cut off Queenie's whisker. Zambini leaned over him, watching closely. This was my chance. I materialised in the cage just behind Zambini and curled the tip of my trunk delicately around his neck and up under his chin. Then I snorted in his ear.

'*NYAAA-A-A-A-A!*' Zambini howled.

Queenie leapt to her feet in an instant, wide awake. Dan tried to get out of her way but she was much too quick for him. Roaring ferociously, she swiped at him with her paw and sent him sprawling against the heavy iron bars.

Before he could make a move to hypnotise her, she sprang. She would have killed him if Zambini hadn't managed, at the very last moment, to grab the end of her tail. Using all his strength, he yanked her backwards just as she was about to sink her teeth into Dan's chest.

Dan tumbled out the door and fell on the grass. Zambini let go of Queenie's tail. Queenie turned and pounced on him but he stepped in and swatted her sideways in mid-air with the back of his hand, sending her crashing into the side of the cage. With a roar loud enough to frighten the dead (and I'm speaking from personal experience here), she got to her feet and leapt at Zambini a second time, but he just managed to get out ahead of her and close the door behind him.

'Holy melted mozzarella,' he gasped. 'That was close.'

'You woke her up, you idiot!' Dan snapped. 'Why'd you have to make that stupid noise?'

Zambini was too bewildered to answer for a second. 'I . . . I see ghost,' he admitted finally. 'I see ghost of Rajah the elephant. He blow een my ear.'

'The ghost of Rajah the elephant blew in your ear?'

'*Si.*'

'That's your excuse, is it? A dead elephant blew in your ear?'

'Ees no excuse. Ees truth.'

'Of all the lame-brained, block-headed . . . I don't believe it! That has to be the stupidest excuse for an excuse I've ever heard! And now look, the entire circus is awake. There are lights going on everywhere! We've got to get out of here!'

Lights were indeed flicking on in some of the caravans. Already a couple of people were running towards us, shining torches over the grass.

'Into the bushes!' Dan commanded. 'Straight ahead – this way! For God's sake, do you always have to *glow* like that? You're a danger to shipping! Can't you turn yourself off?'

'I save your life,' the Great Zambini panted grimly as he ran. 'You no say thank you.'

'*Thank you!*' Dan spluttered beside him. 'For what? For waking Queenie up so she could rip my arms off? I don't think so!'

'That no my fault. I told you, I see ghost.'

'Rubbish. There's no such thing as ghosts.'

'I see ghost of elephant. He blow een my ear.'

'He blow your brains out more likely. *If* he could find any, which I strongly doubt. Now come on!'

7 Plan B

I had successfully foiled a cruel and cowardly attempt on Marvin's life. It wasn't a bad night's work. But that didn't mean I could take a week off and fly to Byron Bay. I had to be on the job twenty-four seven. I knew Dancing Dan would strike again, sooner or later, and I had to be ready.

Over the next few days I stuck to Dan like glue. I followed every move he made, inside his caravan and out. I also kept half an eye on Zambini, who I still didn't trust entirely, despite the fact that he'd said he didn't want Marvin hurt.

It was just as well I did keep watch on Zambini. In the end it was he who gave me my lucky break.

On the morning of the fifth day after the lion's-whisker episode, Zambini got in his car and left the circus. It was risky to leave Dan, but I decided to follow him.

He drove all the way into town and parked outside the library.

The library was definitely not Zambini's favourite hang-out. In fact, as far as I knew, this was the first time he'd ever set foot inside any kind of library in his entire life. Reading made his head throb and his eyes water. It made the few remaining functional parts of his brain work so hard that they began to melt. After a single hour of reading he needed to stop and eat five bowls of pasta sprinkled with steroids, and drink two steaming mugs of Japanese herbal steroid tea, just to get his energy levels back.

That wasn't going to stop him this time, however. He spent all day searching through catalogues and files and indexes before he finally found what he wanted.

This was a very old issue of a magazine called *The Ugandan Women's Weekly*. In the witch-doctoring section at the back was a recipe, which I read quickly over his shoulder:

LION'S WHISKER CASSEROLE

Ladies, if you're ever in the mood for killing your husband, or perhaps getting rid of an irritating neighbour or friend, here's a simple no-nonsense recipe from the jungles of Uganda that will do the job wonderfully well.

Take two or three large lion's whiskers and chop up finely. If you have difficulty getting fresh whiskers you can use frozen — but make sure they are **lion's** whiskers, not leopard's whiskers, or hyena's whiskers, or frog's whiskers, or anything else. Remember that the success of any great dish depends on the quality of the ingredients, and this is no exception.

When you have chopped up your lion's whiskers **very** finely (and ladies — sharpen that knife!) sprinkle them evenly over your beef, chicken or pork casserole. Mix them in well so that no trace remains to the naked eye, reheat, and serve.

After your husband, neighbour or friend has eaten the dish, wait one hour. Your victim will then drop to the floor and begin screaming in agony. This means those wonderful little whiskerettes are puncturing tiny holes in the victim's stomach lining, and causing all sorts of problems down there.

Now sit back and relax. Soon your victim will be stone dead, your whiskers will have completely dissolved in stomach acid, and your only problem will be how to dispose of the body.

I followed Zambini back to the circus after he had finished reading this article. He went straight to

Dancing Dan's caravan and knocked on the door. It was Sunday, one of the circus's nights off, and Dan had finished whatever he'd been doing for the day. He was sitting slumped in an armchair in front of the television, a half-empty bottle of champagne in his hand.

Zambini stormed in and grabbed him by the collar. He lifted him high up in the air with one hand – so high his head bumped against the ceiling – and held him there.

'*Ow!* Zambini! What're you doing?' Dan shouted. 'Have you gone mad?'

'You tell me lion's wheeskors no hurt Marveen,' Zambini said, holding Dancing Dan like a wriggling fish on a hook. 'That no true.'

'It is true!' Dan squealed. 'It is! On my honour!'

'Your *honour!*' Zambini scoffed in disgust. 'What honour ees thees? You have no honour! You nothing but a rat crawling een a snake's belly! I no be friends weeth you no more!'

He dropped Dan in a heap on the floor and stormed out, slamming the door so hard that he ripped it right out of its frame.

Then, a few seconds later, he burst in again.

'I warneeng you now, Dan,' he said. 'You hurt Marveen again, I keell you. You touch-a heem again,

I keell you. You talk-a heem no nice, you laugh-a heem, you make-a no-nice face . . . *eef you do any-theeng to heem I no like, I keell you! Hokay?*'

Dancing Dan didn't answer. His face had gone a sickly grey and his Adam's apple was bobbing in his throat. He remained in a heap on the floor till long after the Great Zambini had gone. Then he crawled back into his armchair and painfully dusted himself off.

'Right,' he muttered to himself. 'If that's the way you want it, fine. Who needs you anyway, you overgrown sea-slug? You're so dumb you make tree stumps look smart. I've met inflatable pool toys with a higher IQ than you. I'll get the little Gumbo brat without you, and I won't *have* to touch him. I'll just use Plan B. If I could just come up with the right gimmick, the right new trick . . . It's time to put on the old thinking cap, Daniel my boy, and let that famous creative genius flow . . .'

He found a pen and some paper amongst the piles of rubbish scattered around the room, then sat back in his chair. He began feverishly writing notes, scribbling things out, writing things down again, mumbling and cackling to himself all the while.

'Yes . . . yes . . . of course, that's brilliant . . . No, don't be stupid. It'll never work. It's got to be bigger . . . more spectacular . . . a real extravaganza: something so good that Colin Gumbo wouldn't *dream* of turning it down. Think, Dan, think. Your entire circus career is at stake . . .'

Twice in the space of half an hour he stood up, wildly excited. Twice he sat down again, bitterly disappointed. He worked till well after midnight, when the floor around him was littered with scrunched-up bits of paper.

The third time he stood up, a crazed light of triumph burned in his eyes.

'Yes,' he croaked hoarsely. 'Of course. It's exactly what I'm looking for. The kid could never match that, not in a million years. Not if he kissed his own bottom wearing a suit of armour and swinging from a chandelier. If I can pull this off, he'll be a nobody again. Colin Gumbo will be at my mercy. And the Gumbo Circus Royale will be mine, all mine . . .'

The following morning, after waking from a refreshing one-and-a-half hours' sleep, Dan got ready to go out. He dressed in his cleanest (or should I say least filthy) lion-tamer's suit, combed six months' worth of spilt champagne out of his hair, and shaved. When he had made himself look as smart as he possibly could, he set out across the compound to pay a visit on Colin Gumbo in his office.

'Sorry to burst in on you like this,' he said in his most charming, friendly tone, after Colin Gumbo let him in. 'It's just that . . . well, I've been racking my brains recently, thinking of ways we could improve our wonderful circus . . . and I think I've come up with a bit of an idea.'

Colin Gumbo wrinkled his nose. He hadn't been this close to Dancing Dan for a long while, and, to be perfectly honest, Dan stank. It wasn't just that he stuck his head down lions' throats all the time, for a bath in rotten meat breath. It was also that he'd given up washing. He hadn't had a bath or a shower for months, not since the first night Marvin had performed.

'Have you brushed your teeth recently, Dan?' Colin asked.

'My teeth?' Dan looked puzzled. 'Of course I have! I brushed them . . . let me think . . . not last month, but the month before.'

'When was the last time you had a haircut?' Colin Gumbo went on.

'A haircut?' Dan spluttered. 'I had . . . I mean, I have haircuts all the time, I—'

'You're a wreck,' Colin Gumbo said. 'Look at you. Your hair's a rat's nest. Your skin's the colour of frozen pavlova. Your teeth look as if they've been soaking in paint stripper for a year.'

'I didn't come here to talk about my teeth,' Dancing Dan said.

'No, you've probably come here to demand more money,' Colin sighed. 'That's what you usually come here for. Unless it's to complain about Marvin.'

'Well, now that you— I mean no, of course not! Why would I want to complain about Marvin?' Dan smiled an oily smile. 'He and I are best friends! We're practically blood brothers! It nearly broke my heart when the poor child stopped performing after Rajah died. Seeing him become successful again has made me truly happy.'

Colin Gumbo's eyes narrowed. 'Just what *have* you come here for, Dan?' he asked.

'I want to put on a new act,' Dan said. 'It'll mean a lot of extra work, rehearsing and so on, but I'm not asking for any more money. All I want is some publicity. When I'm ready to perform I want the whole world to know about it. I want my name – and the name of the Gumbo Circus Royale, of course – plastered everywhere. On every billboard. In every newspaper and magazine in the country.'

'So you *are* asking for more money,' Colin Gumbo said. 'That'll cost a small fortune.'

'You'll earn it back,' Dan said. 'A hundred times

over – no, a thousand. What I'm planning to do makes juggling horses and kissing bottoms look like playtime at the local pre-school.'

'So what *are* you planning to do?' Colin Gumbo asked.

'Ah.' Dan smiled mysteriously. 'I want to keep it a secret. That's part of the plan.'

'What plan?'

'The plan to get publicity. I'll hire out an empty warehouse in town and rehearse there. No one will be allowed inside – just me and my lions. At the same time we'll issue press releases saying that I'm working on the show of the century. We'll leak a few wild rumours to whet the press's appetite . . . we'll say that I'm dressing my lions in tutus, and that they're rehearsing *Swan Lake*, or something like that. Once the ball starts rolling the public will be bursting with curiosity. It'll be huge.'

Colin Gumbo nodded. He could see it might work. Dancing Dan was a total scumbag, but when it came to lion-taming, he knew his stuff better than anybody. If he said he had a fabulous new act, he had to be taken very seriously.

For this 'mystery act' gimmick to work, though, the act would have to be *really* fabulous. There was nothing worse than whipping the public into a frenzy about something and then have it turn out to be a fizzer.

'So you're asking me to back this idea of yours, and spend a small fortune on publicity, when I don't even know what the act is,' Colin Gumbo said. 'I take it you're *not* dressing your lions in tutus and rehearsing *Swan Lake*.'

'No, of course not.' Dan smiled again. 'It's *much* better than that. It's far and away the best idea I've ever had. Trust me!'

8 The Great Comeback

Soon rehearsals on Dancing Dan's new show were in full swing. Every morning at eight o'clock Dan hitched his lions' cages up to one of the circus trucks, and drove them to a warehouse in town. He rehearsed for five hours, took a break for lunch, then returned in time to get ready for that night's show.

No one else was allowed inside the warehouse. Anyone who tried to get in was turned away politely but firmly by two security guards stationed at the door.

Colin Gumbo, true to his word, promoted the new show heavily. He bought half-page ads in national newspapers, and ran commercials on prime-time TV, at enormous cost. He also paid for posters and billboards to go up all over the city, and sent a press release that Dan had written himself to thousands of media outlets all around the country.

LION-TAMER PLANS MYSTERY COMEBACK! the press release said. SHOW OF THE CENTURY PROMISED AT GUMBO CIRCUS ROYALE!

One of the great circus performers of the modern era, Dancing Dan the Lion-tamer, is set to make a spectacular comeback. Dancing Dan is at this very moment rehearsing a secret new show at a warehouse at an undisclosed location in the city.

The show is so secret that not even the circus owner, Colin Gumbo, knows all the details. But according to the handsome and swashbuckling maestro himself, it will put other circus performances so far in the shade they'll be growing mushrooms.

'Believe me, baby, this new act is the real thing,' the daredevil hero said. 'It's hotter than hot. Nothing else comes close.'

Looking healthy and relaxed in his spotless luxury caravan, the heart-throb hypnotist denied that he was dressing his lions in tutus and rehearsing Swan Lake.

'There is absolutely no truth to that rumour,' he said. 'What I'm planning is far more spectacular. My new act will make Disney on Ice look like clean-up time at the teddybears' picnic. So be there or be square!'

The date for the grand premiere was set for the beginning of August. A week before the big night, Dan surprised everybody by demanding that all the sawdust inside the Big Top be removed, and that the ring be concreted over instead.

'What!' Colin Gumbo exclaimed. 'I can't do that! It'll cost a mint! And besides, it'll be dangerous! What if one of the Gumbo-ettes falls off the back of an elephant? What if Knuckles bungles his high-dive, and misses his bucket? His head'll split open like a melon!'

'They're professionals,' Dancing Dan said. 'They wouldn't make mistakes like that.'

'Everybody can make mistakes sometimes,' Colin Gumbo said. 'Even you.'

'Well, of course' – Dan grinned slyly – 'if you want to throw away all the money you've already spent on publicity, go ahead. Without the concrete, my act can't go on.'

Colin Gumbo was furious, but he had no choice. He'd spent so much money on Dancing Dan's new act that he would be ruined if it didn't go on. So he ordered the trucks in, and replaced the sawdust with concrete that afternoon.

As everyone counted down the days, Dan got busier and busier. He bought himself a brand-new black velvet lion-tamer's outfit, complete with boots and a whip. He finally went to the barber and got himself a haircut – and dyed all the specks of grey out of his hair. Then, with only two days to go, he released his very own rap song, which was so terrible that it can't be reproduced here, except for the first verse:

I'm Dancing Dan! I'm the Man who Can!
I've got Plans for the Fans! I ain't no Also-Ran!
My Game is to Tame! I'm the Big Name with all
the Fame!
I Tame the Cats that Kill and Maim, so Listen to
my Claim!

Finally the day of the grand premiere dawned, cloudy and drizzly. After breakfast, Marvin made his way to the Big Top for his usual morning rehearsal, but to his surprise the entrance was locked. Knuckles the Clown, Chubby Cupcakes and the Great Zambini were standing in a huddle on the grass, looking cold and wet and frustrated.

'Why are you all out here?' Marvin asked.

'We been shut out!' Zambini exclaimed. 'Baneeshed from our own-a tent, like dogs!'

'Dan says he needs to have the ring to himself,' Chubby Cupcakes said. 'All morning. So he can run through a full dress rehearsal with his lions.'

'But what about the rest of us?' Marvin said. 'That's not fair! We haven't got used to the concrete yet.'

'He's acting as if he owns the place,' Knuckles grumbled. 'It might be his grand premiere, and all that, but we're performing too. What are we supposed to do?'

'I no rehearse, I no perform!' Zambini fumed. '*Finito!* I go back-a my caravan and watch-a *Sesame Street!*'

Just as Zambini was leaving, Colin Gumbo arrived, and did his best to calm everyone down.

'I know it's unusual, but it's only a one-off,' he explained. 'Dan needs a dress rehearsal in the ring, and his show's meant to be a secret, so obviously we can't go in. It'll be all over by lunchtime.'

'And meanwhile, we get to stand around in the rain,' Knuckles the Clown said. 'Brilliant.'

'I'm telling you, this whole thing's got disaster written all over it,' Chubby grumbled.

At six o'clock that evening, the gates to the compound opened. The crowd began to pour in steadily. All the performers gathered as usual back-stage, where they mingled with the circus hands and the animals.

The only person missing was Dan. He wasn't there at six-thirty either. Colin Gumbo grew more and more anxious with every minute that went by.

'Where *is* he?' he asked Knuckles. 'I haven't seen him or his lions since he finished rehearsing.'

'Oh, he's around,' Knuckles said. 'You know these big superstar types. They don't want to hang out with nobodies like us.'

By seven o'clock Dan still had not arrived. Colin Gumbo was beside himself, but he couldn't wait any longer. It was time to start the show.

On the other side of the curtain, under the Big Top, the air was electric with anticipation. Six thousand people were squashed in shoulder to shoulder, while hundreds more without tickets had been turned away at the door.

The crowd hushed as a simple white spotlight cut through the darkness in the middle of the ring. It illuminated the proud figure of Colin Gumbo, dressed in his ringmaster's top-hat and tails.

'*Ladiiiiiiiies and gentlemen!*' Colin Gumbo boomed. '*Welcome one and all, old and young, rich and poor, to the wonderful, the magical, the truly sensational GUMBO CIRCUS ROYALE!!!*'

An almighty roar went up. The music surged. Coloured lights burst overhead like fireworks. The circus hands led all the animals and performers – except Dancing Dan, who was still nowhere to be seen – in the first grand parade of the evening.

When the parade was over, everyone took a bow and left the ring. Only the two Indian elephants, Daisy and Nellie, remained behind. Two circus hands ran out and blindfolded them. A drum roll began, and slowly grew louder.

With a clash of cymbals and a blast of trumpets, Olwyn Gumbo burst through the half-open curtains. She sprinted towards a springboard in the centre of the ring. Halfway across she began tumbling, turning flips and cartwheels, never once changing direction or slowing down. She hit the springboard feet first, shot high into the air, and flipped three more times before landing upright, perfectly balanced, in the middle of Nellie's back.

Next, the nine other Gumbo-ettes ran out. Four of them leapt to a standing position on Daisy's back. As Daisy blundered sightlessly around the ring, three more Gumbo-ettes leapt off the springboard. They timed their jump to perfection, landing on the other four Gumbo-ettes' shoulders. The last two Gumbo-ettes repeated the trick, landing on the three Gumbo-ettes' shoulders, so that now only one spot on the very top of the pyramid remained.

Nellie and Daisy continued to lumber around the ring, with the human pyramid on one and Olwyn Gumbo on the other. Olwyn waited until the elephants were just the right distance away from each other, and leapt. She performed a flawless triple backwards flip with a double sideways twist, and landed exactly on top of the pyramid with her arms raised in triumph.

The crowd roared.

'*Ladiiiiiies and gentlemen!*' Colin Gumbo's voice boomed. '*Would you please welcome to the ring the high-flying, awe-inspiring, death-defying team of tumblers, holder of six world records, voted best circus performers in the known universe by* National Acrobatic *magazine, the one, the only . . . OLWYN GUMBO AND THE GUMBO-ETTES!*'

After Olwyn and the Gumbo-ettes it was the Great Zambini's turn. He began by juggling ten blazing firesticks at once, tossing them so high they left smoke marks on the top of the tent. Then he juggled plates and rings and ping-pong balls, before finishing with the most amazing act of all: the horses.

A hush always went over the crowd when Zambini juggled horses. Nobody could quite believe what they were seeing. This was the one trick that

Marvin always tried to sneak a peek at through the curtains, if he could manage it. The sight of the three fully grown thoroughbreds looping and tumbling through the air never ceased to fill him with awe.

Before Zambini left the ring, he lay on his back and juggled three large porcelain vases with his feet. This was the signal for Knuckles and his monkeys to come on. Knuckles swaggered into the ring with an enormous cream pie, which he threatened to throw at the audience. Then he tiptoed over to Zambini, while Zambini was still juggling the vases, and tossed the pie right in his face.

Zambini leapt to his feet with cream dripping from his moustache. The three vases smashed on the ground. Knuckles laughed uproariously, then, while Zambini was still wiping away the cream from his moustache, he took out his harmonica and began playing to the crowd. Zambini tiptoed up behind Knuckles, whipped his harmonica out of his hands, and tossed it to the monkeys, who climbed with it to the diving platform and out along the high wire.

Knuckles chased after the monkeys until one of them dropped the harmonica, and he retrieved it. Then the monkeys went after *him*. After a breathless pursuit Knuckles plunged from the high dive, dropping forty metres into half a bucket of water. He emerged sopping wet and smiling, with the harmonica still in his hands.

Chubby Cupcakes was next. She performed her famous trapeze routine, scaring the audience witless with her bombing raids from on high. After she was done, Colin Gumbo entertained the crowd with his magic act, finishing off as he always did by pulling a live fire-breathing dragon from his underpants.

Then, all too soon, it was Marvin's turn. Watching him walk out into the ring, I have to admit I was nervous. I had no idea how he would handle the pressure. What if his famous elastic spine froze up, and he was stuck forever with his head between his legs? What if nerves gave him an upset stomach? What if an unexpected bubble of gas escaped at just the wrong moment, and he was forced to inhale his own fart?

In the end I needn't have worried. Marvin's performance was fantastic. He got a standing ovation. I almost wished I could appear, right there and then, to carry him around the ring in triumph, but I didn't want to give myself away just then, so I simply hovered invisibly nearby.

Marvin walked out through the curtain with the wild cheers of his fans still ringing in his ears.

Waiting on the other side of the curtain, with his lions, was Dancing Dan.

'Hello, pipsqueak,' Dan said with a sneer. 'Enjoy yourself out there, did you? I hope so. Because amateur night is over now. Time for the professionals to take charge.'

Dancing Dan snapped his fingers. His four lions got to their feet. They weren't on leashes. Only Dan's amazing hypnotic powers kept them from attacking whoever they pleased.

Then, all at once, Marvin noticed what was different. He gasped. He stared, and kept on staring.

The lions were on rollerskates. Dan was too. Dan didn't look so odd, because he always wore large black boots. These simply had wheels attached underneath. But the lions looked totally ridiculous. All four of the great beasts had a sleek, black, state-of-the-art titanium rollerskate strapped to each paw.

They also looked unwell. Weeks of rehearsals had left them exhausted and thin. As Marvin watched in horror, one of them – it was Queenie – got up and skated gracefully in behind Dancing Dan.

'Rollerskates!' Marvin breathed. 'So that's your new act! But you can't put lions in those! They'll damage their paws!'

'Oh really?' Dancing Dan said, and cracked his

whip. At once the other three lions skated in a long slow arc behind Queenie. 'So who's going to stop me? You?'

Out in the Big Top, a drum roll sounded. The crowd quietened as the spotlight fell once more on Colin Gumbo in the middle of the ring.

'*Ladiiiiiiiiies and gentlemen!*' Colin Gumbo cried. '*At long last, the moment you've all been waiting for! The Gumbo Circus Royale is proud to present the circus entertainment event of the century! You've read the posters! You've seen the billboards! You've listened to the ads and the interviews and sung along to the rap song! Now it's time to welcome the world's most celebrated animal hypnotist, the dedicated, the debonaire, the devil-may-care lion-taming genius . . . DANCING DAN!!!*'

The curtains were flung open. The crowd erupted. Just before he made his long-awaited grand entrance, Dan turned to Marvin.

'This act is going to make me a superstar, pipsqueak,' he said. 'And do you know the first thing I'm going to do, after I become mega-huge? I'm going to ruin you. You *and* your miserable parents. I won't rest until this circus belongs to me, and all three of you are eating mouldy old hamburger wrappers out of the gutter. Now *get out of my way!*'

Marvin stumbled aside as Dan and his lions swept

73

past. He and I watched helplessly as the lions began skating in a circle around the ring. The people in the crowd were so flabbergasted they forgot to cheer. They simply stood with their eyes frozen open and their jaws hanging.

Marvin snapped into action. He ran as fast as he could to the dressing-room caravan, not far from the rear exit, where his mother was putting on fresh make-up for the final farewell parade.

'Mum, Mum!' he shouted as he burst in. 'We've got to stop the show! Dancing Dan's sworn to ruin us, and destroy everything!'

'Calm down, Marvin, calm down,' Olwyn Gumbo said. 'What's going on?'

Marvin explained as quickly as he could, repeating Dan's oath word for word.

'He really said that?' Olwyn asked. 'He said we'd be eating mouldy old hamburger wrappers out of the gutter?'

'Yes! He's out to get us! We've got to stop the show!'

'I knew that slimy bucket of dog-spit was up to no good,' Olwyn Gumbo said. 'But we can't stop the show, Marvin. Only the ringmaster can do that. And no ringmaster has ever stopped the Gumbo Circus Royale in two hundred years.'

'I've got to tell Dad! I'm going out there!'

'Marvin, you can't! Dan's act has already started! The lions—'

But Marvin was already running back to the ring, with me floating just behind him. There an amazing sight met our eyes. Dancing Dan was whirling under the spotlight, cracking his whip fiercely above his head, while around him his four lions skated a series of high-speed zig-zags, pirouettes and figure-eights.

While they did this, four circus hands came out carrying a heavy wooden ramp. Another four followed, wheeling a metal base on which stood three giant hoops. One of the circus hands turned on a gas burner hidden inside the base, and all three of the hoops burst into flame.

'And now, ladies and gentlemen!' Colin Gumbo announced, 'Prepare yourselves to witness the impossible! A spellbinding leap through not one flaming hoop, not two flaming hoops, but THREE FLAMING HOOPS, all standing five metres above the ground! This is an act of feline acrobatics that no other lion-tamer could even dream of! Take it away, Dan!'

Dan cracked his whip. Queenie began skating at top speed towards the ramp. She soared through the first two hoops with ease. The flame at the base of the third hoop burned the tip of her tail, making her yowl, but she landed strongly.

Princess followed. She cleared all three hoops cleanly. So did Empress and King. After they'd finished their jumps, all four cats joined Dancing Dan in skating a lap of honour. The audience cheered and cheered.

Marvin ran to his father, out of the spotlight. 'Dad!' he called. 'Dad, listen to me! You've got to stop the show!'

Colin Gumbo switched off his microphone. 'Marvin! What are you doing here? We're in the middle of a show!'

'You've got to stop it, Dad! Dan's going to ruin us! He's going to destroy everything we've worked for!'

'Stop the show? Don't be ridiculous! I can't do that!'

'He's out to get us! I heard him say it! Dad, *please*!'

'No Gumbo has ever stopped a show and I won't be the first!' Colin Gumbo said gruffly. 'Now go! We can talk about this later!'

'Later will be too late!'

'Go!'

He turned his back. Marvin walked away, dejected.

The lions' next trick was a forward jump with a somersault in mid-air. No lion had ever performed a somersault before, let alone one in mid-air, on rollerskates, after flying off a ramp. If Dan's lions completed this trick successfully, his status as a circusing superstar would be assured.

The first three lions executed their jumps perfectly. When King's turn came, the flash of a camera in the audience distracted him. He didn't get nearly enough height on his jump. He flipped over in mid-air and came down heavily on his side, where he lay growling softly.

Everyone gasped. Marvin could hardly bear to watch. Just as the circus hands ran out to help, King got up again. He shook his mane groggily, gave a feeble roar, and staggered back towards Dan.

'Stop the show now, Dad, please,' Marvin muttered. 'This is crazy. Dan's gone way too far.'

But Colin Gumbo did nothing of the kind.

'Ladies and gentlemen!' he announced. 'You've all seen lion-tamers put their heads into lions' mouths. You've all heard of the famous "Tonsil Tickler", pioneered by our very own Dancing Dan. But now, ladies and gentlemen, you will see something even more breath-taking. Something so dangerous, and intricate in its timing, that it could only be performed by one man. The Gumbo Circus Royale presents the final act of the evening . . . perhaps the greatest circus act of all time . . .

77

DANCING DAN'S TONSIL TICKLER ON SKATES!'

Dan made all the lions sit in a row. He skated slowly in front of Princess, waving his hands hypnotically. As soon as she yawned, he clicked his fingers. Princess's mouth froze wide open. Dan lowered his head, spread his arms out wide, as if they were wings, and glided forward in a single smooth motion, until his head disappeared completely down Princess's throat.

The crowd roared. Dan took his head out, blew kisses to his fans, then got ready to do the same thing with Queenie.

It was then that I noticed Queenie's tail.

While Dan had been blowing kisses to his fans, Queenie had flicked her tail out in front of her. It now lay directly in Dan's path. I'm sure she hadn't done this on purpose. She was so heavily hypnotised she probably didn't even remember that she *had* a tail.

Dan hadn't seen it yet. He was too busy trying to put her to sleep. Right on cue, Queenie gave an enormous yawn and Dan clicked his fingers, freezing her mouth wide open.

Just then Marvin saw the tail too. 'He's going to hit it!' he said out loud. 'He'll skate in and hit it, right when . . . *Dan! No, don't! Look out!*'

His shouts were lost in the roar of the crowd. Before he could call out again, or run to help, it happened.

Dancing Dan lowered his head, and spread out his arms. With a flick of his heels he skated forward, aiming right in between those two rows of razor-sharp, powerful teeth, and right over Queenie's tail . . .

9 Dan Loses His Head

There's no easy way to describe what happened next. It was horrible, even for me, and I've witnessed my own death.

Just as Dancing Dan's head disappeared into Queenie's mouth, his rollerskates bumped over her tail. Queenie let out an ear-splitting yowl. She bit down hard, and sliced Dan's head clean off.

It happened so fast that at first nobody noticed. For a second or two, Dan's body remained exactly where it was. Then his arms dropped, his knees buckled and he collapsed to the ground.

Queenie got up groggily and walked away. She was still carrying Dan's head in her mouth. She rolled it around on her tongue for a while, like a large uncooked brussels sprout. Then gently – oh so gently – she opened her jaws and dropped it onto the floor.

Pandemonium broke loose. Grown men fainted. Women screamed. Children covered their eyes and hid under the seats. Thankfully, at that very same moment, a very clever and quick-thinking circus hand hit the emergency light switch, and the entire Big Top was plunged into darkness.

'Call a doctor!' I heard somebody shout.

'Call the police!'

'Call an ambulance!'

'Sew his head back on!'

'Keep calm! Don't panic!'

'Get those cats back to their cages!'

It was chaos. Any moment now there would be a full-scale mob riot. Marvin hurried to find his father, who was kneeling in the darkness beside the headless body of Dancing Dan.

'Dad, you've got to make an announcement!' Marvin said. 'People are frightened! You've got to calm them down!'

Colin Gumbo stared numbly at the body in front of him. 'He's dead, Marvin,' he said. 'Dancing Dan is dead. And I'm the one who killed him.'

'What are you talking about? Queenie's the one

who bit his head off, not you! You weren't anywhere near him!'

'I never should've let the show go on. I should have stopped it. I should've checked what Dan was doing. This whole thing was a disaster waiting to happen, just as Chubby said.'

'Dad, the crowd!' Marvin waved towards the stands. 'They're panicking! They need to know what's going on!'

But Colin Gumbo didn't move. He remained on his knees with his head bowed and his face in his hands. Marvin decided to act. He reached down and unclipped the small radio microphone attached to his father's collar.

He clipped the microphone to his own collar, and switched it on. *'Ladies and gentlemen,'* he said. *'May I have your attention, please. This is Marvin Gumbo speaking. My father can't talk to you right now, so I am speaking on his behalf, and on behalf of everyone at the Gumbo Circus Royale. Quiet, please.'*

The crowd calmed. They couldn't see Marvin in the darkness, but they could hear him perfectly.

'Ladies and gentlemen, there's been a terrible accident,' Marvin went on. *'The great lion-tamer Dancing Dan is dead. I'm sure you understand that the show has to be stopped. The police will be here soon, and we'll have to*

help them with their enquiries.

'We are all very upset that this has happened. Dan was part of our circus family. He was loved by fans all over the world. Maybe we should remember that he died doing what he loved best, in front of the people he loved most — you, his loyal fans. Thank you, and have a safe journey home.'

After Marvin finished, the crowd began leaving. There was no panic. Soon the stands were empty. Only the circus hands and the performers remained.

Fifteen minutes later the police arrived. They began interviewing everyone except Colin Gumbo, who was still too upset to speak. An ambulance drove into the Big Top, and two ambulance officers carried away Dancing Dan's body in a zip-up bag.

Knuckles and Chubby and Zambini stood with Marvin as the ambulance drove off. The sight was too much for Zambini. He broke down in tears.

'Why he put hees lions on-a rollerskates?' Zambini said. 'Why? Why?'

'I guess some people just don't know when to quit,' Knuckles said.

'That was a great speech you gave for him, Marvin,' Chubby said. 'We all know he didn't deserve it. He was nastier to you than to any of us, and he was cruel to his animals as well. It's hard to know what to say about a man like that.'

'I like to remember the good things about him,' Marvin said. 'When I was a kid I loved watching him perform. He really was a fantastic lion-tamer. Probably the greatest the world has ever seen.'

After breakfast the following morning Olwyn Gumbo asked all the performers and circus hands to meet outside the Gumbos' caravan. When everyone had arrived, she opened the caravan door and helped her husband down the steps.

Colin Gumbo looked dreadful. He had aged twenty years overnight. His eyes had lost their sparkle, and were sunk deep into their sockets.

'My friends,' he said sadly, 'thank you for coming. I won't keep you long. You've all been with the Gumbo Circus Royale for many years now, through good times and through bad. I think you will agree that this is our darkest hour.'

'Our colleague Dancing Dan has left us,' Colin Gumbo went on. 'He has gone to join that great three-ringed circus in the sky. I have called you here this morning to tell you that I take full responsibility for what happened.'

'No! No!' everyone cried. 'It was an accident!'

Colin Gumbo held up his hand for quiet.

'I appreciate your loyalty, dear friends,' he said. 'But certain things can't be ignored. It was I who let

Dan rehearse his new act in secret. Not once did I check on him during rehearsals. Not once did I ask him for details. I trusted him – as I would trust any of you – to keep the best interests of the Gumbo Circus Royale at heart, and in doing that, my friends, I made the biggest mistake of my life.'

'Last night,' Colin Gumbo continued, 'I learned that Dan had sworn an oath to ruin Marvin and destroy our family circus forever.'

Colin paused, then went on: 'Dan may be dead, but I'm afraid he has succeeded in his aim. The rest of our season has been cancelled, leaving us deep in debt. Also, our licence to keep animals has been cancelled. Because of what happened last night, we can no longer keep lions, or elephants, or monkeys – not even horses. The heart and soul of our circus has been taken away. This spells the end for the Gumbo Circus Royale, and once again, I take full responsibility. I hereby resign as owner and ringmaster. From now until the circus disbands, my son Marvin and my wife Olwyn will be in charge. Thank you and good day.'

A stunned silence greeted this speech. Marvin looked just as shocked as everyone else.

'You can't resign, Dad!' he exclaimed. 'It's your circus! And none of this is your fault!'

'It's over, Marvin,' Colin Gumbo replied. 'There's

no hope. I've failed you, my son. I've failed you all.'

With that, Colin turned and began shuffling up the steps back into his caravan. Olwyn Gumbo rushed to his side.

'Dad, Dad!' Marvin pleaded. 'You can't do this! We need you! It was a mistake, that's all. Everybody makes mistakes.'

It was no use. Colin Gumbo shut the caravan door. With tears in his eyes, Marvin turned to face the circus hands and performers.

'I don't know exactly what's happening yet,' he said, 'but could you please give us one more month? If we haven't sorted everything out by then, and got the circus back on track, you can start looking for other jobs. Is that too much to ask?'

Chubby Cupcakes came slowly forward on her forklift. 'Of course not, Marvin,' she said. 'A month is fine. Isn't that right, everyone?'

Everyone murmured agreement.

'I guess the first job is to get the Big Top down, and all the stands packed away,' Marvin said. 'Then we'll have to deal with the animals. But the main thing is not to give up. If we stay optimistic and keep hoping, you never know what will happen. I refuse to believe we're beaten! I just *won't* believe it!'

10 Two Meetings

For the rest of that day, Marvin stayed inside the
Gumbo family caravan with his parents. Everyone
else began taking down the Big Top and packing
it away. As for me, I spent half my time hovering
miserably above Marvin inside the caravan, wishing
I could cheer him up, and half my time hovering
miserably above the Big Top, wishing I could help
there. To be honest, I had no idea *what* to do with
myself.

Or why I was even still here.

The only reason I'd become a ghost was to
protect Marvin from Dancing Dan. As soon as Dan
died, I should have begun slowly fading away. There
are no free rides in the afterlife. You don't get to stay
on in the mortal world after your job is done.

So what was I doing still hanging around like a bad smell? The more I thought about it the more puzzled and worried I became. It just didn't make sense.

Unless . . .

My suspicions were confirmed later that evening, after everyone had gone to bed. I was floating past the performers' caravans on my way to my old cage, when I sensed something. It was vague at first – the faint tingling of tiny vibrations, drifting through the cool night air.

I stopped, confused. The vibrations seemed to be coming from the direction of the caravans. I swerved that way a little bit, and yes – the vibrations grew stronger.

Then they stopped.

It was as if they were holding their breath, waiting for me to pass.

I knew then that I had stumbled on another ghost. I also knew that the other ghost had stumbled on *me*. Now we had no choice but to confront each other, to find out what we were doing on each other's territory.

I swooped as fast I could towards Dancing Dan's empty caravan. As I got closer I could feel the vibrations increase, until they became a loud buzzing roar all around me.

Get out! Get away! This is my territory! I heard Dan's voice snarl. *Back off, hose-nose! One step closer and you'll be elephant burgers!*

Something came out through the wall of the caravan just in front of me. It was shapeless, an angry red mist that glowed with a dark and evil energy.

Like two old-time cowboys in a Western, we faced each other across the grass.

Why are you still here? I asked.

The same reason you are, Dan said. *I swore an oath. I promised I'd ruin Marvin, and I won't leave until the job's done.*

And I won't leave until he is completely safe — from you, anyway, I said. *Which means only one thing, pardner. This circus ain't big enough for the two of us.*

You're right. I suggest you pack your bags and leave on the next train, before I suck you up through a straw.

There was no escape for either of us. We were bound by our oaths to engage in a fight to the finish. (I was about to say a fight to the death, but that wasn't exactly true, considering that we were both already dead.)

You didn't plan all that with Queenie, did you? I asked. *Rollerskating over her tail, getting your head bitten off and so on. Surely you weren't THAT desperate!*

Of course I didn't plan it! Dan snapped. *It was an accident! If I hadn't been killed in such a stupid and humiliating fashion, I'd be a superstar by now!*

Oh how the mighty are fallen, I said, and gave a ghostly elephant chuckle.

Dancing Dan glowed redder than ever. *Go ahead and laugh. You'll be laughing on the other side of your face when the circus is ruined and the Gumbos are out on the street.*

Don't count on it, Dan. It hasn't happened yet.

And who's going to stop it? Marvin? Now it was Dan's turn to chuckle. *That lily-livered little jelly-baby? He couldn't stop a sneeze if he was holding his nose.*

He faded away suddenly, and I continued back to my cage. If Dan left his caravan at any time to go after Marvin, I would sense it and be on him in a flash. But I had a feeling he wouldn't. Right now everything was going perfectly for him. The circus was about to be ruined anyway. All he had to do was sit back and watch.

The next week was one of the saddest times I'd had at the circus. It was the week that the animals began leaving. The first to go were Zambini's horses, which were sold to a riding school out in the country. The lions left next, on their way to a large safari park in Africa. Knuckles' monkeys were shipped back to

Madagascar, while Nellie and Daisy were taken to a reserve in northern India.

The circus felt empty and abandoned without them. It was exactly as Colin Gumbo had said it would be. The heart and soul of the place had gone. A few days later the cages went too – sold to another circus – and the mood of depression deepened.

Only one cage wasn't sold, and that was mine. The Gumbos wanted to keep it, to honour my memory. So it stayed exactly where it was. Late in the evening, Marvin would come and lie quietly on the straw.

Sometimes I would appear to him, and he would talk to me about how things were going.

'Dad's not good, Raj,' he said to me one night. 'He's given up on everything. He just lies in bed and does nothing, twenty-four hours a day. He keeps saying the circus is ruined, there's no hope left. Mum is at her wits' end trying to look after him. I wish I could give them some good news.'

But you can, I thought, and vanished. A moment later I reappeared on the outside of my cage. My sensitive ghostly antenna had picked up something happening on the far side of the compound that Marvin needed to see.

I banged gently on the door of the cage with my

trunk. Marvin came out and stood beside me, puzzled.

'What is it, Raj?' he said. 'What's up? You want to take me somewhere?'

I flapped my ears and trumpeted softly.

'It's a bit late for a ride, isn't it?' Marvin said. Then, when I began stamping my feet impatiently, he said, 'All right, all right, don't get your tusks in a tangle. I'm coming.'

He climbed up on my shoulders and off we went, heading for the Great Zambini's caravan. No light was on inside the caravan, but a small fire was burning in a clearing behind it. Around this fire sat Zambini, Knuckles, and Chubby – perched as usual up on the front of her forklift.

All three were deep in conversation. None of them had spotted us yet. Before any of them could turn around, I passed quickly in front of Zambini's caravan and out of sight.

'Did they send you to get me, Raj?' Marvin whispered. 'No, I don't think they did. Not if you're making such an effort to stay out of sight. This is a secret meeting, isn't it? One I'm not supposed to know about. So what d'you want me to do now, climb up on the roof and listen?'

That was exactly what I wanted. I raised my

trunk and tapped it against the edge of the caravan roof, which was only just higher than the top of my head. Marvin stood on my back and climbed up.

He slithered on his stomach to the far side, where he could see the three circus performers easily and hear every word they said. By this time I had vanished again, and was hovering just above him.

'No, no, no!' Zambini was saying animatedly to Knuckles. 'You no understand! Eef I joggle you, Knuckles, maybe I drop you! Maybe you land on your head!'

'So what?' Knuckles shrugged. 'Can't be worse than diving forty metres head-first into a bucket.'

'What about Marvin?' Chubby asked. 'Could you juggle him as well?'

'Marveen!' Zambini chuckled. 'That leetle peep-a-squeak! I joggle heem on my leetle peenkie feenger, like thees!'

'Good,' Chubby said. 'Glad to see you're so confident. And how about me? Could you juggle me as well as the other two?'

Silence settled like a shroud of doom around the fire. Zambini looked thunderstruck. All the colour drained from his face.

'Mamma mia,' he mumbled. 'Holy melted mozzarella. You no say notting about thees.'

'You need three people, that's the whole point,' Chubby said. 'It's got to replace your act with the horses. I guess you could always juggle Olwyn, if she was willing. But imagine the headlines if you could juggle me. *WORLD'S STRONGEST MAN JUGGLES WORLD'S FATTEST LADY*. It would be fantastic. It's exactly what we need to get the new Gumbo Circus Royale off the ground.'

The Great Zambini chewed on his moustache. He seemed to be glowing a lot less brightly than usual.

'I no sure, Chobby,' he said. 'I joggle horses, *si*. I joggle cows. I joggle three leetle peegs and the beeg bad wolf. But I never joggle *notting* like you.'

'What d'you think I am, a Sherman tank?' Chubby glared at him. 'I'm not *that* fat! Come on, let's try it right here and now.'

Slowly, with the greatest reluctance, Zambini got to his feet. He looked at Chubby and gave a heavy sigh.

'Hokay,' he said. 'I joggle you now, or I die trying. But probably I die.'

'That's my boy!' Chubby said. 'Lift me up, you big hunk of spunk! Be the wind beneath my wings! Toss me in the air like confetti!'

'No worries, Zambini!' Knuckles called out. 'It's a cinch! She's light as a feather!'

The Great Zambini drew himself up to his full height, and sucked in a series of deep, energising breaths.

'I *theenk* I can, I *theenk* I can, I *theenk* I can . . .' he said.

'Go, Zambini, go!' Marvin whispered below me, from the rooftop of Zambini's caravan. 'You can do it! You can do it easy!'

With a tremendous grunt of exertion, Zambini lifted Chubby into his arms. With a second tremendous grunt he raised her high above his head, where he held her for a few seconds at full stretch, getting ready to throw her into the air.

The weight was almost too much for him. His face went purple. Glowing blue veins pulsated on his mighty biceps. His knees shook. His arms wobbled. I felt sure that his strength would give out at any moment, and both he and Chubby would collapse to the ground.

Then, with a roar like a runaway train, he tossed Chubby five metres straight up in the air.

He braced himself as she came down again. 'Goodbye, Mamma,' he said tenderly. 'Goodbye, Pappa. Goodbye, leetle bambinos . . .'

He caught her.

In one hand.

He tossed her up into the air a second time, and caught her in the *other* hand when she came down again.

'*You did it!*' Chubby exclaimed, as Zambini tossed her a third time, and she turned a somersault in mid-air. 'This is *much* better than the trapeze! This is *wonderful!*'

'I drop you!' Zambini wailed. 'I no strong enough!'

'Oh, stop whining! You could keep this up all night!'

For the fourth time, a four-hundred-and-fifty-nine-kilo human cannonball dropped down on Zambini. Finally his strength gave out. He crumpled to the ground with his face pressed hard into the grass, and with Chubby lying flat across his back.

'Excellent,' Chubby said as she rolled off him and climbed back onto her forklift. 'Your technique needs work, and your muscle tone's a bit sloppy. But not bad at all for a first try.'

'*Uhhhhh-h-h-h,*' Zambini groaned. 'I deezy. Every-teeng go faint. Every bone in my body she broken.'

Zambini managed to get to his knees and crawl halfway to his caravan before he collapsed a second time. He lay face-down in the grass again.

'A bit more practice, a few more steroids in his spaghetti, and he'll be chucking me around like a football,' Chubby said to Knuckles. 'Now, what about you, mate? How are we going to do your comedy act without the monkeys?'

'I know the answer to that!' Marvin said, and stood up suddenly. 'We use the Gumbo-ettes! They can steal Knuckles' harmonica and chase Knuckles around just like the monkeys! The audience would love it!'

He jumped down on the grass between Chubby and Knuckles, narrowly missing Zambini's head.

'Marvin!' Chubby exclaimed. 'Marvin, what are you doing here?'

'Listening to you! I heard everything! You're trying to invent new acts without animals, so the circus can keep going!'

He turned to face Zambini, who had struggled onto his knees, and threw his arms around the strongman's neck.

'Zambini, you were great! You caught her in one hand! I saw you! *In one hand!*'

'Mamma?' Zambini croaked. 'Mamma, ees that you?'

'But how did you know we were meeting here?' Chubby said. 'We didn't tell a soul! We didn't want to let you in on our plan until we knew that it could work!'

'Rajah told me,' Marvin replied. 'He's here, watching the whole thing. He's the one that brought me.'

'Rajah?' Chubby frowned. 'What – you mean *our* Rajah? Rajah the elephant?'

'Yes!' Marvin said. 'Well, I mean – his ghost, obviously. Not the real Rajah. He must have known what you were doing from the beginning.'

'You're joking, aren't you?' Chubby said. 'Or have you *really* been visited by Rajah's ghost? You *have*? Oh, that's wonderful!'

'Poor kid's kissed his own bottom one too many times,' Knuckles muttered to Zambini. 'I knew it would get him in the end.'

'Be quiet, Knuckles!' Chubby said. 'If Marvin says he's seen Rajah's ghost, I believe him one hundred per cent! I've seen a few ghosts too, in my time. Rajah's obviously been sent to look after you, Marvin, which is the best news we've had in ages.'

Zambini crossed himself. 'I no like ghosts,' he said. Then suddenly a look of shocked recognition came over his face, and he gave a loud gasp.

'Rajah!' he said. '*Si!* I remember now! He blow een my ear!'

'You've seen him too?' Marvin asked.

'*Si, si!*' Zambini could hardly control his excitement. 'Weeth Dan! I thought I go crazy! But he save your life, Marveen! He make me stop Dan from doing a very bad theeng!'

'You see?' Chubby said to Knuckles. 'Zambini's seen him too. They can't *both* be wrong, can they?'

'A twelve-year-old kid and an Italian on steroids?' Knuckles said. 'You want to bet? Besides, all that superstitious mumbo-jumbo means nothing to me. I only believe what I see with my own eyes.'

'Then look behind you,' Marvin said. 'Over there, by the trees.'

Since everyone was talking about me, I decided I might as well join the party. I appeared on the other side of the fire. My ghostly grey shape was flickering eerily in the light from the flames. It was a pretty impressive entrance, if I may say so myself, and it caused quite a reaction. Chubby gave a squeal of delight. Zambini sank to his knees and began saying prayers. Knuckles blinked once, swallowed thickly, then fainted.

'C'mon, you guys!' Marvin laughed. 'It's not the Virgin Mary! It's only Rajah!'

'He's beautiful!' Chubby said. 'Look at him! He looks so *real*!'

'You can touch him if you like,' Marvin said.

But as the three of them moved towards me,

I vanished again. What Marvin didn't realise was that Chubby and Zambini *couldn't* touch me – not the way he could. Only he could ride on my back and pat me and so on, because it was him I'd come to protect.

'He's gone.' Chubby signalled to her forklift driver to stop. 'That's such a shame. I wish he wouldn't go.'

'He hasn't gone,' Marvin said quietly. 'He's still here. He's *always* here. And you definitely saw him, didn't you?'

'Definitely,' Chubby nodded.

'*Si*,' Zambini agreed.

'So did Mr Tough Guy over there,' Chubby added, pointing to Knuckles, who was still out cold on the grass. 'And I'll make sure I remind him of it, about ten times a minute, after he comes round.'

11 An Amazing Recovery

I kept watch outside Dan's caravan for the rest of the night, but paid Marvin a visit early the next morning. He was already dressed and eating breakfast. As soon as he'd finished, he went to his father's bedside and woke him gently.

'Hm? Wha—? Wossat?' Colin Gumbo shifted on his pillow and blinked. 'Go away. I'm dying.'

'Morning, Dad,' Marvin said cheerfully. 'It's a beautiful day outside. Why don't you come out with me and take a look?'

Colin Gumbo gave a long, mournful sigh. 'No, Marvin my boy,' he said. 'I've seen all I want of life's hollow pageant. I'm happy to let the rest pass me by.'

'I really think you should come outside, Dad. It's *such* a great day. Be a real shame to miss it.'

'No, no, no, no.' Colin Gumbo closed his eyes and settled back onto his pillow. 'You and your Mum go on out. I'll just lie here and suffer.'

'Sorry, Dad,' Marvin said firmly. 'There's something I need to show you, and I won't take no for an answer.'

Colin Gumbo opened one eye cautiously. 'Hm?' he mumbled. 'What did you say?'

Marvin leaned out the caravan door and whistled. 'Zambini!' he shouted. 'Dad's not being very co-operative! He needs a bit of gentle persuasion!'

'Eh?' Colin Gumbo opened both eyes wide, and sat up. 'What d'you mean, gentle persuasion? What're you talking about?'

'*Buon giorno*, Signor Gombo!' Zambini beamed as he squeezed his massive frame in through the Gumbos' front door. 'Ees a wonderful morning, no? Perfect for the leetle show we do for-a you today!'

'Show? What show? What's going on?'

'Ah, ees a beeg surprise!' Zambini laughed. '*Molto* entertaining! *Molto* extraordinaire! But first, we make you all nice and comfy, *si*? For today, you our guest of honour.'

He reached out to take Colin Gumbo by the arm. Colin Gumbo shrank back against the wall.

'Are you mad?' he said. 'I'm sick! I'm desperately ill! I can't leave my bed even for a minute!'

Zambini nodded. 'Hokay,' he said. 'No worries. Eef you can't leave-a your bed, we take-a your bed too.'

Without another word Zambini leaned across Colin Gumbo's mattress and picked it up. He rolled Colin Gumbo up inside it like a sausage in a giant sausage sandwich.

'Help!' Colin Gumbo shouted. 'Olwyn, do something! Zambini's gone berserk! He's turning me into a tortilla!'

Zambini glanced at Olwyn Gumbo, who was sitting at the breakfast table, calmly sipping a cup of tea. He gave Olwyn a wink.

'I take heem now, Signora Gombo?'

'Be my guest,' Olwyn Gumbo said. 'And don't be in a hurry to bring him back, either. Keep him out there all day if you want. The fresh air will do him good.'

'Fresh air!' Colin Gumbo squawked. 'I don't want fresh air! It's dangerous! My lungs are too delicate!'

'There's absolutely nothing wrong with you, and you know it,' Olwyn Gumbo said. 'You're acting like a spoilt, good-for-nothing child, and it's got to stop!'

As Colin Gumbo continued to protest, Zambini

swung him around and guided him head-first through the open door.

'Aaaah! The sun! The sun!' Colin Gumbo wailed. 'It's blinding me! It's melting my eyeballs!'

'I put you in the shade, no worries,' Zambini said.

'Don't put me anywhere! Take me back to bed! I'm dying!'

Zambini turned to Marvin, who smiled. Olwyn Gumbo appeared in the caravan doorway behind them with her arms folded.

'On second thoughts, you can leave him out here all week,' she called. 'Do him good.'

Colin Gumbo's jaw dropped. 'You can't leave me out here all week, my little jacaranda blossom,' he said weakly. 'It might snow!'

'Good! I hope it does!' Olwyn said. 'I hope you get buried under a snowdrift ten metres deep! Then maybe you might decide you don't want to die after all!'

'We just want you to watch us for a while, Dad,' Marvin put in. 'Take a look at our new show.'

'Your show!' Colin Gumbo grumbled. 'Fine time to put on a show, when all our animals have gone, and the circus is as good as ruined!'

Marvin didn't bother to argue. He put two fingers in his mouth and gave a loud whistle. From behind the row of caravans to his left, Chubby Cupcakes' forklift appeared. Chubby was on the front of it, and walking beside her was Knuckles the Clown.

Following these two were the Gumbo-ettes and all the circus hands. They stood to one side while Knuckles, Chubby and Zambini took up positions directly in front of Colin Gumbo, on a flat stretch of grass.

'*Ladiiiiiies and gentlemen!*' Marvin announced. '*What you are about to see is a sneak preview of the greatest juggling act the world has ever known! It is only the first of many exciting new routines planned for the Gumbo Circus Royale! Forget Dancing Dan and his lions! Forget monkeys and horses and elephants, and everything you've seen in the past! This, friends and neighbours, is the sleek, streamlined, super-charged circus of the future!*'

He bowed, then went to stand beside Zambini, who was nervously chewing on his moustache.

'I no sure I can do thees, Marveen,' Zambini whispered.

'Sure you can,' Marvin whispered back. 'You had your triple helping of steroids for breakfast, didn't you?'

Zambini nodded.

'And your ten-stack of steroid-flour pancakes, and your steroid-and-banana smoothie?'

'*Si.*'

'Then you've got nothing to worry about.'

After checking that everyone was in position, Chubby's driver pressed the extension button on his forklift. The twin forks underneath Chubby rose to a height of ten metres, then stopped. Chubby stepped to the very edge of her platform, and gave Zambini a teasing wave.

'Yoo-hoo!' she called. 'Hello down there, big boy! I'm ready when you are!'

Zambini gulped. 'Holy melted mozzarella,' he mumbled to himself. 'Leaping lasagna. Why I agree to do thees?'

'It's for the circus, Zambini,' Marvin whispered to him. 'It's for all of us. This will be your finest hour!'

Zambini steadied himself. He nodded to Chubby, then bent down and stuck out a hand. Marvin stepped on it. Zambini then hoisted Marvin high above his head, and in one effortless movement tossed him high into the air.

Marvin did a double backwards flip with a half-twist. He landed perfectly on Zambini's hand. He performed more flips and twists, and then finished by doing a handstand on Zambini's shoulders.

Knuckles stepped up onto Zambini's other hand. He too was hoisted up and tossed high into the air. Then, as if it were the most normal thing in the world, Zambini began juggling Marvin and Knuckles, catching them each time they fell, and hurling them upwards again with great sweeps of his powerful arms.

Colin Gumbo got slowly to his feet. He stood on his mattress in his pyjamas, watching in stunned fascination. His wife and the rest of the small crowd applauded wildly.

'Bravo!' Olwyn Gumbo called out. 'Bravissimo! More! More!'

With a nod of his head, Zambini signalled to Chubby. She leapt from her forklift. Zambini caught her one-handed, held her, and tossed her skywards again. Not only that, but he managed to keep juggling Marvin and Knuckles at the same time.

'Oh my God!' Olwyn Gumbo gasped. 'That's impossible! No one could be that strong! Did you see that, Colin? *Did you see it?*'

'I saw it! I saw it!' Colin Gumbo jumped up and down on his mattress like a kid on a trampoline. 'It's unbelievable! It's the most marvellous act I've ever seen!'

Zambini's face was a picture of concentration. He was tiring now. Sweat was running down his face, dripping off his ears and nose. But still he kept juggling. The three bodies – one small, one medium, and one extra-extra-large – kept spinning and whirling and tumbling over each other, making fantastic loop-the-loops in the air.

Finally Zambini's strength gave out. One at a time he caught Marvin, then Knuckles, then Chubby, and lowered them to the ground. He stood facing Colin Gumbo, exhausted and gasping for breath. All four performers gave a low bow.

'It's a miracle!' Colin Gumbo shouted, as he jumped even higher on his mattress, his eyes shining with delight. 'It's awe-inspiring! It's a guaranteed, sure-fire hit! Olwyn, my darling! Call the circus hands! Unpack the trucks! Put up the Big Top! How long have we got before our next season of performances?'

'We don't have a next season of performances,' Olwyn said.

'*What?!* Why not?'

'We've cancelled all our bookings.'

'But that's madness!' Colin Gumbo exclaimed. 'That's completely insane! Who's the clump-headed clotbrain that gave the order to do that?'

'You, Dad,' Marvin said.

'Well, I'm giving another order! I order you to re-book the bookings! Fax the dates! Send off the publicity! Check the equipment! Don't just stand there gawping, everybody! Move it! We've got WORK to do!'

12 Something in the Fridge

The change that had come over Colin Gumbo was quite extraordinary. After a good hearty breakfast, a shower, a shave, and a change of clothes, he was as good as new. He spent the rest of that day striding purposefully around the compound, barking orders and encouragement to the performers and the circus hands as they busied themselves putting up the Big Top.

'That's it, everyone! Steady as she goes! Careful with those poles!'

Marvin was delighted that his father was well again, but I knew it meant trouble. Now that the circus was back on its feet, Dancing Dan would have to come out of hiding. He would launch an all-out war on the Gumbos, and especially on Marvin, trying to destroy the circus for ever.

The first attack came the very next day. Marvin had been working with his parents all morning, and was heading back to the Gumbos' caravan for lunch.

He climbed the steps and raised a hand to open the front door. As soon as he touched the handle, it started vibrating and became red-hot — so hot that smoke began rising up from it. Marvin let go of the handle with a yell and stepped back off the steps — which was just as well, because without warning the caravan door flung open and slammed hard against the outside wall.

A loud humming noise was coming from inside the caravan. A bright white glow shone out through the open doorway. It was as if the whole place had turned into a giant lightbulb.

'No need to panic,' Marvin said to himself. 'There's got to be a logical explanation. It must be a power surge.'

Yanking the door open, he quickly dived inside. At once the humming noise inside grew deafening. The white glow grew so bright he could hardly see. Paintings banged against the walls. Cups dropped from the table and smashed. Marvin had to grab hold of the corner of the kitchen bench to stop himself from tumbling over.

The bright white glow was coming from the

fridge – a small bar fridge set under the far end of the kitchen bench, next to the table.

Marvin swung the fridge door open. A blast of freezing air rushed past him, nearly knocking him off his feet. The caravan shuddered and bucked underneath him.

Suddenly everything stopped. The noise died down and the caravan went deathly still. Marvin held his breath a moment, then slowly opened his eyes.

In the fridge, lying in a bowl of leftover potato salad, was the head of Dancing Dan.

The head was staring straight at Marvin. It was covered in creamy mayonnaise and small chopped-up lumps of potato.

It grinned.

'Hello there, pipsqueak!' it said, in a harsh, gurgling voice. 'Are you hungry? What can I get you? Some potato salad? A glass of milk? A stick of celery from the vegetable drawer?'

'Dan!' Marvin gasped.

'Dancing Dan the Lion-tamer at your service. Only I'm not dancing as much as I used to. Or taming lions, for that matter. Hard to do that sort of thing when you don't have arms or legs.'

'But what happened to them?' Marvin asked. 'Where's the rest of your body?'

'My body!' The head scowled furiously. 'Don't talk to me about my body! If I ever see that clumsy, knock-kneed bag of chicken bones again, I'll tear it limb from limb! I mean honestly – rollerskating over a lion's tail! Have you ever heard of anything so stupid? And it had to do it right when I was sticking myself inside the lion's mouth, too, didn't it? It couldn't skate around the tail, or jump over it – oh no! It had to roll right smack-dab over the middle! It didn't even try to save me from being bitten off, the traitor!'

'I don't think it had much of a choice,' Marvin said. 'The whole thing happened so fast. There wasn't time to do anything.'

'Well, you would say that, wouldn't you?' the head sneered. 'I know whose side you're on.' It began to swell slightly. Its eyes glowed a deep, evil red. 'I see you are preparing a new show,' it said menacingly. 'New acts. New performances. Performances without *me*.'

'Well, yes, but you're dead,' Marvin said. 'We can't help that.'

'That's no excuse!' the head snapped. 'Don't you realise my death marked the end of the Gumbo Circus Royale for ever? I *am* the circus! You can't put on a new show without me! I absolutely forbid it!'

As it spoke these words, the head blew itself up like a pufferfish, until it filled every corner of the fridge. With a twitch of its neck, it sent the bowl of potato salad crashing to the floor. It opened its mouth and let loose a blast of foul, stinking demon-breath, aimed straight at Marvin. Marvin staggered and dropped to his knees, coughing and spluttering desperately, gasping for air.

I had to do something. I tried to materialise, so I could engage the head in battle. But to my horror, I found I couldn't. I couldn't change from being invisible to being visible again. Some unknown force was stopping me, holding me back.

Another blast of demon-breath hit Marvin. One more would probably finish him off. Choking and gagging, he began crawling towards the front door. All I could do was hover, invisible and useless.

The head gazed down contemptuously at Marvin.

'That's it, you little worm!' it shouted. 'Crawl! Crawl for your life! Go and tell the others what you've seen! Tell them that if they dare to put on another show without me I will destroy them utterly! I will turn the Gumbo Circus Royale into a chamber of horrors! No one will be spared!'

13 The Haunting

As soon as Marvin could stand up again, he went to find his parents. I followed, still invisible, feeling desperate. If I couldn't figure out how to materialise again before opening night, all was lost. Dan was far too strong for any of the circus people – even the Great Zambini – to fight on their own.

When they heard Marvin's story, Colin and Olwyn Gumbo came straight away to check out the caravan. It was a shambles. Pictures had fallen off the walls. Cups lay smashed under the table. The fridge was making a strangled chugging noise, like a car engine about to run out of fuel. Just as the Gumbos arrived it gave a clunk and a gurgle, and chugged its last.

'Look at my kitchen!' Olwyn Gumbo burst out. 'It's a disaster zone!'

'Now, Marvin,' Colin Gumbo said, 'tell us exactly what happened.'

'I've already told you what happened! It was the head of Dancing Dan! He was in the fridge, and he got bigger and bigger, and . . .'

'All right, all right, don't get upset.' Olwyn Gumbo patted him on the shoulder. 'We believe you. Don't we, Colin?'

'It sounds to me like the Bungling Brothers, all over again,' Colin Gumbo said.

'The Bungling Brothers?' Marvin said.

'They were two clowns who decided to start their own circus, back when I was a boy,' Colin Gumbo said. 'They built it into the biggest and most famous circus on earth. Their star attraction was a strongman named Gastromo, who could eat anything. Car tyres. Metal pipes. Chunks of granite cut from a quarry. At every performance he would challenge the audience to bring him something that he couldn't eat.'

'He offered them money, too,' Olwyn added. 'A thousand dollars if he couldn't take at least one mouthful of what they brought him, and swallow it. That was a lot of money in those days.'

'So what happened?' Marvin asked.

'Ah, it was a terrible thing,' Colin Gumbo said. 'A worker at an atomic energy plant brought in a lump of irradiated plutonium. He didn't tell Gastromo what it was. He simply walked out of the audience, wearing a full anti-radiation body-suit, and handed it to him. Gastromo munched it up like a Snickers bar, then gave an almighty belch, and announced that it tasted great. Five minutes later, when he was halfway through eating a packet of disposable razors, he dropped dead.'

'But it was the plutonium that killed him,' Olwyn added. 'Not the razors.'

'Absolutely,' Colin Gumbo said. 'They did an autopsy on him that same night, and couldn't find his stomach. They looked everywhere – under his heart, in between his kidneys, behind his ears. A team of expert surgeons searched for that stomach for sixteen hours, but it had completely disappeared.'

'And *then*,' Olwyn Gumbo went on, 'Gastromo returned to haunt the circus. He blamed the Bungling Brothers for not protecting him from the plutonium. He said they should have warned him that it might be damaging to his health. Just before he died, he vowed revenge on the circus, and in six months the Bungling Brothers were ruined.'

'How?' Marvin asked. 'What did Gastromo do?'

'What d'you think?' Colin replied. 'He ate everything. He ate the entire Big Top from top to bottom.

Then he ate the trucks, and the caravans, and the cages, right down to the last nut and bolt. The Bungling Brothers' insurance policy didn't cover them for having their circus eaten by a ghost. They couldn't afford to buy new equipment, and so they were ruined.'

There was a silence. Then Marvin said: 'Dan gave me a warning after he attacked me. He told me that if we dared to put on a new show without him, he would destroy it. And destroy us as well.'

'I thought so,' Colin said. 'He's vowed revenge, just like Gastromo. Now we *are* in a stew.'

'I think we should go and see Chubby,' Olwyn said. 'Straight away.'

'Why Chubby?' Marvin asked.

'Chubby's mother was a fortune-teller as well as a trapeze artist,' Colin explained. 'So Chubby grew up schooled in the Dark Arts. She's seen a few ghosts in her time, and she knows quite a lot about them. If anyone can help us deal with Dan's ghost, she can.'

The three of them found Chubby in the yard outside her caravan, doing exercises on her forklift. When she did chin-ups, she stood on the forks of the forklift and instructed the driver to raise her up slowly, until her chin cleared the top of a nearby tree branch. When she did push-ups, she lay face-down on the ground with the forks underneath her, and instructed the driver to lift her up by her stomach.

Every day she did a hundred chin-ups and a hundred push-ups without moving a single muscle. It was a wonderful exercise program. She had even written a book about it, entitled *The Forklift: Your Key to Advanced Physical Fitness*, which was on sale wherever all good books were sold.

When the Gumbos arrived she had just completed her hundredth push-up and was ready to take a break.

'Colin! Olwyn! Marvin!' she said. 'What's up?'

Colin Gumbo explained quickly about Dancing Dan. By the end, Chubby looked extremely worried.

'I agree with you that we're in deep trouble,' she said. 'There's nothing worse for a circus than being haunted by an angry ghost. It's all right for an old abandoned farmhouse, or for an empty castle that nobody visits. But a circus like ours is a hive of activity. Imagine what will happen if Dan's head *does* come back to haunt us on opening night. There'll be a stampede. People could get killed.'

'We were wondering,' Olwyn said, 'if you knew of any way we could protect ourselves. Colin said you'd had a bit of experience with this kind of thing.'

'The only sure-fire way to get rid of a ghost,'

Chubby said, 'is to have another even more powerful ghost get rid of it for you.'

'Like Rajah!' Marvin exclaimed. 'You said before that you thought he'd come to protect me! Now we know why!'

'Rajah?' Colin Gumbo said in surprise. 'What's he got to do with anything?'

'Don't tell me his ghost is here too,' Olwyn Gumbo said.

'Yes, it is.' Chubby frowned. 'I've seen it myself. So have Knuckles and Zambini. But what puzzles me is why Rajah didn't help Marvin just now, when Dan appeared in your caravan. If Rajah *is* here, and he *has* sworn to protect Marvin, he should have been all over Dan like a rash.'

Exactly! I thought. *The trouble is, I can't do anything! I'm like a rabbit waiting to be pulled out of a hat!*

'Maybe he couldn't get there in time,' Marvin said. 'It all happened pretty fast.'

'No, ghosts are much quicker than that.' Chubby smiled. 'And besides, with Dan around, Rajah will be shadowing you wherever you go. He'll be here now, listening to this very conversation, I'm sure of it.'

She paused a moment, looked around, then called out, 'Rajah! Rajah, if you're here, show yourself! Give us a sign!'

I was desperate to do just that, but I couldn't. I was still trapped helplessly in my invisible form. The only thing I could do was swoop down and swirl up a few dead leaves lying on the grass in front of the forklift. Even that left me feeling woozy and exhausted.

'There! Did you see that?' Chubby said. 'Those leaves! That's him!'

'It was definitely something,' Olwyn Gumbo admitted. 'But I don't think we can beat Dan by stirring up leaves.'

'Why doesn't he just appear the way he did at Zambini's?' Marvin said angrily. 'What's the point of staying invisible? Especially when he knows we need him so badly!'

'I don't think he *can* appear,' Chubby said. 'I think there's something wrong. What did you do the last time he appeared, Marvin? Where were you?'

'In his cage,' Marvin answered. 'I go there sometimes at night, just to be alone and think. That's where he always appears first.'

'Good,' Chubby said. 'Go there again tonight. Do everything that you normally do. Don't change a thing. I've got a feeling it's *us* that's causing the problem, not Rajah or Dan. If we do everything right – and that means you, Marvin, because he's your guardian angel – I'm sure he'll come.'

14 Earth Calling Rajah

Listening to Chubby had given me new hope. If what she said was true, and the problem wasn't with me, but with Marvin — or maybe with the circus itself — then that could easily be fixed.

But what could the problem be? I racked my brains trying to think of it. I'd never heard of anything like this happening to another ghost. The only thing that could make a ghost lose its power to appear was its home disappearing or being demolished. That was an ancient, unbreakable rule known to all ghosts, and which we were forbidden to ever reveal to mortals.

It was the perfect explanation, except that my home — my sturdy old elephant cage — was still exactly where it had always been. Therefore, there was no way the rule could apply to me.

Marvin was just as puzzled as I was. Late that night he came out to my cage to try and summon me, but after he got inside and closed the door he had no idea what to do. He didn't normally light candles, or say a prayer, or sing a song, or anything like that. He usually just sat there doing nothing, and after a while I appeared.

So he sat, doing nothing with all his might, while I hovered outside. I was positively bursting to make myself visible, and when I couldn't, I got more and more frustrated. *Everything's the same!* I thought to myself. *Everything's just the way it should be! So why can't I do it? Why? Why?*

It was a cold night – winter was well and truly upon us by now – and Marvin wore gloves, a beanie, tracksuit bottoms and a scarf as well as his jacket. He was doing his best to stay warm, but already he looked half-frozen. I knew he couldn't stay in my cage for too long.

At midnight he switched on a torch that he'd brought with him, and shone it around the grounds.

'Raj,' he said, 'I know you're out there somewhere. I know you're listening, too. We need you to come back, Raj. We need you more than ever before. You're the only one who can help us, and if you don't come, we lose everything. All our hard work! All our hopes and dreams! The opening night will be a disaster, and the circus will be completely destroyed!'

It was agony not being able to answer him. I wanted so much to be there beside him, to reassure him that I'd protect him when the new show opened.

But I couldn't.

I couldn't do anything at all.

Marvin waited another five minutes. Outside the cage, nothing stirred. Not a breath of wind, not a leaf, not an insect.

'Raj,' Marvin said again, shivering miserably, 'I can't stay here much longer. My toes are going numb. I don't know how to do this, and you're not making it any easier. Why don't you save us both a whole lot of hassles, and show yourself?'

Once again I couldn't answer. Marvin lost his temper. He whacked his hand hard against the floor of the cage.

'Come *on*, Rajah! You're doing this on purpose! You're doing it just to torture me!'

Straight away he put both hands up to his face and shook his head. 'I'm sorry, I didn't mean it,' he said. 'You know I didn't. You're the best friend I've ever had. I just need you to come.'

I hovered miserably, only a few metres away.

I don't think I've ever felt as bad as I did then. To make matters worse, just at that moment I sensed a familiar tingling somewhere off in the distance – a sign that Dancing Dan was once again on the move.

Hardly had the tingling started when a blood-curdling scream pierced the air. It was followed by a loud clattering noise, and the smashing of glass.

'Zambini!' Marvin leapt to his feet. 'That was Zambini screaming! Oh no!'

He scrambled out of the cage and ran towards Zambini's caravan, with me hovering close behind. When we arrived, we could hear Chubby's forklift starting up somewhere in the distance. Knuckles and Colin and Olwyn were already there.

Zambini was outside on the grass in his pyjama-bottoms, swinging a golf club wildly above his head, and talking to himself in a loud incoherent babble. Steam was coming off his arms and shoulders.

Behind him, both of the front windows of his caravan were smashed to pieces.

'*Stay back!*' Zambini howled. '*Keep away! I warning you!*'

He swung the golf club so hard that he spun around and fell over. Just then Chubby arrived, followed by two of the circus hands, and most of the Gumbo-ettes.

'He's seen something,' Olwyn muttered to Colin, as Zambini got back on his feet. 'Something scary. You didn't tell him about Dan, did you?'

'Of course not,' Colin replied. 'Seeing the ghost of Rajah was hard enough for him. If he thinks he's seen the ghost of Dancing Dan, he'll go mad.'

Zambini looked worse than after he'd juggled Chubby. His body was damp with sweat and his eyes were wild.

'I send you back to Hell, you monster!' he shouted.

'Zambini!' Colin called to him. 'Zambini! It's me, Colin Gumbo! You're safe now! Nothing's going to hurt you! Put the golf club down!'

Zambini blinked at Colin uncomprehendingly. Like a child caught stealing something from a shop, he put the golf club down. Colin ran forward and took it from his hands.

'I see heem!' Zambini croaked. 'I am asleep, and he come to me! He float above my bed! Weeth the beeg sharp teeth, and the burning red eyes! I no see nothing like thees before, never!'

'It was just a dream, Zambini,' Olwyn Gumbo said. 'I know it was horrible. But it was just a dream.'

'No, no, no! Thees was no dream! It was Dan! Just hees head, no his body! He tell me I going to die!'

Zambini dropped to his knees. Olwyn and Colin Gumbo glanced at each other in alarm.

'It *was* only a dream, Zambini,' Chubby Cupcakes said firmly. 'I can prove it. What did you have for dinner last night? Apart from steroids, I mean. Did you have any mushrooms? Fettucine funghi, maybe?'

'No, no fettucine funghi,' Zambini said. 'Seafood. Spaghetti marinara.'

'Ah, seafood!' Chubby nodded. 'There you are then! That explains everything! Prawns, was it? Oysters? Baby octopus?'

'Octopus, *si*. But—'

'Well, *of course* you're seeing heads floating above your bed!' Chubby exclaimed. 'The octopus was off! It was rotten! It was probably months old! You're lucky you haven't got food poisoning as well!'

Zambini thought this over. 'Maybe the marinara she do taste a leetle strange,' he admitted. 'But the head! He so real! He talk to me, just like Dan!'

'Ah, a *talking* head,' Chubby Cupcakes nodded as if this was exactly what she'd expected. 'That means *two* baby octopuses must have been off. Or one baby octopus and three prawns. Or one baby octopus, two prawns, four oysters, and a fish cocktail. Either way, the effects will have worn off by now. You're going to be perfectly okay.'

With much fussing and cajoling, Chubby and Colin managed to herd the Great Zambini back into his caravan. Knuckles offered to stay with him for the night, to keep him company in case he had any other bad dreams. Zambini gratefully accepted.

'That was *brilliant*, Chubby,' Colin Gumbo said, after Knuckles had closed the door. 'For a minute there I thought it was all over. I thought Zambini was going to pack up his bags and leave.'

'He'll never leave,' Chubby said. 'He loves the circus too much. But we've got to do something about Dan before *all* of us start seeing heads. Marvin, did you have any luck with summoning Rajah?'

Very quickly, Marvin explained what had happened.

'There must be *something* we can do,' Olwyn Gumbo said. 'What if we brought him some food? Some donuts, maybe? They always used to be his favourites.'

'Ghosts don't eat food,' Chubby said. 'But it's worth a try.'

'Maybe Rajah isn't hearing Marvin properly,' Colin Gumbo suggested. 'He was very old for an elephant, you know. He was going a bit deaf when he died. Perhaps if Marvin spoke into a loudspeaker . . .'

'All ghosts have excellent hearing,' Chubby said. 'Even deaf ghosts.'

'Then why isn't Rajah here?' Marvin asked. 'If he can hear me, and see me, and understand what I'm saying, what am I doing wrong?'

'I don't know the answer to that,' Chubby said. 'But I *do* know we've only got two nights left. We've got to try everything we can think of – and I mean *everything*. There just has to be a solution to this problem, and one way or another we've got to find it.'

The next day Marvin spent rehearsing with the other performers in the Big Top. Zambini was there, and seemed no worse for his experience the night before. All the concrete in the ring had been removed, and replaced with good old-fashioned sawdust, which everyone much preferred.

After the rehearsals, Marvin helped his parents, Chubby and Knuckles to repaint my old cage. Colin Gumbo ordered three buckets of jam donuts to be delivered from a cake shop in town. He bought a brand-new CD of my favourite circus music, and put a CD player in my cage so Marvin could play it. He filled a wheelbarrow with flowers and apples and peanuts and bread rolls and cold meat pies, and hung balloons and streamers from the top of the cage, along with a banner saying 'RAJAH – YOU ARE STILL THE ELEPHANT OF OUR DREAMS'.

'Is that enough?' he asked the others when this was done. 'Can you think of anything we've missed?'

'What about the costumes Rajah used to wear?' Olwyn Gumbo said. 'The head-dresses, the elephant saddles, the ankle bracelets and so on?'

'Brilliant! Those are in one of the big bins, with all the other animal equipment. Go and find them.'

So Olwyn went and got my old performing costumes, which were wonderfully bright and glittery and filled with coloured glass and ostrich feathers and things like that. She laid them out in my newly painted cage underneath the banner, next to the CD player and the wheelbarrow full of fruit and nuts and pastries and flowers, and the buckets full of fresh jam donuts.

'Now that looks beautiful,' she said proudly, when the display was finally finished. 'What more could a dead elephant ask for?'

'If the old stewed prune doesn't come tonight, he'll never come,' Colin Gumbo said, but Chubby only shook her head.

'The ways of the spirit world are forever mysterious to us mere mortals,' she advised.

'In other words,' Knuckles said, 'we still don't have a clue what we're doing.'

'At least we're not *fainting*,' Chubby said stiffly,

causing Knuckles to go red. 'At least we're doing *something*.'

So, at midnight, poor Marvin made his next lonely pilgrimage out to my cage. Once again he was dressed in his jacket, tracksuit, gloves, beanie and scarf, for the night was just as cold. Once again he'd brought his torch, and this time he'd also brought his father's loudspeaker, just in case I'd gone deaf.

'I feel like a goose coming out here with all this stuff, Raj,' he muttered, as he settled himself on the fresh straw next to one of the buckets of donuts. 'I'm sure this isn't the answer. You don't need music or donuts or costumes to make you come back and help me, do you?'

He waited. A fog was beginning to roll in off the ocean, shrouding everything in a thick blanket of white.

'Maybe some music will cheer me up,' he said, and switched on the portable CD player beside him. A loud burst of cheerful circus music filled the air. He let it play for ten seconds, then clicked it off again.

'You're here inside the cage with me, aren't you?' he said. 'You're so close I can feel you. What are we forgetting, Raj? If it's something so vitally important, why can't we think of it? I'll bet you don't know what it is either, do you, mate? Even if you could talk, you couldn't tell me.'

I hovered only a metre away from him, completely helpless.

Marvin picked up his father's loudspeaker. 'May as well give this a blast,' he said, and switched it on. '*Earth calling Rajah,*' he announced. '*Earth calling Rajah. Attention all ghost elephants. Come in, please. Your time is up.*'

It didn't work.

Nothing worked.

I was just as invisible as I had been before.

The fog continued to roll in slowly, covering the cage, the caravans and the Big Top in a frosty white haze.

15 Showtime!

By morning the fog had lifted. The day dawned clear and calm and sunny. It was the perfect day for the grand premiere of the New Gumbo Circus Royale – weatherwise, at least.

In other respects, the outlook for that evening's performance wasn't quite so good.

'I wonder if he'll appear at the beginning of the show or at the end,' Marvin said gloomily to his parents at breakfast. (No one sitting at the table that morning – or hovering above it – needed to be reminded who 'he' was.)

'At the beginning, I'd say,' Olwyn Gumbo said. 'He won't want the show to get going. People might start enjoying themselves.'

'He might choose to keep us in suspense for

a while,' Colin Gumbo said, 'then make a grand entrance, just when we least expect it. He'll do that better if he comes at the end.'

Three forks poked listlessly at three plates of cold bacon and eggs.

'Look, Marvin,' Colin Gumbo said. 'I don't want to put *pressure* on you or anything. But are you sure you've given this business with Rajah your best shot?'

'Oh Colin, leave him alone,' Olwyn said. 'He's been through enough already.'

'No, I will not leave him alone!' Colin Gumbo said. 'He's the one who grew up with the mangy brute! He's practically an honorary elephant himself! If *he* can't figure out what's happening, no one can!'

'We've been through this before,' Olwyn Gumbo said firmly. 'It's not Marvin's fault and I don't want you to blame him. Now finish your breakfast.'

Colin Gumbo poked at his bacon and eggs again. They were now so cold they were beginning to turn blue.

'Maybe Rajah doesn't like us doing a show without animals,' he went on. 'Or maybe he doesn't like me being in charge again. That could be it, don't you think? He preferred it when Marvin was in charge, and now he's gone off in a huff.'

'He's not like that, Dad,' Marvin said. 'He

wouldn't let Dan ruin us just because he's in a huff. And he doesn't care that we don't have animals – he was the one who took me to see Chubby and Knuckles and Zambini, when they were planning their new acts in secret. He *wants* to come back and help, but he can't. I can feel it. He's just as much in the dark as we are.'

'Well, he's *your* guardian angel,' Colin Gumbo grumbled. 'You'd think you might know.'

At ten in the morning all the performers gathered in the ring for a rehearsal. Everyone put on a very brave face, but a vague feeling of doom hovered over the proceedings, like heat before a storm. In the middle of the afternoon Marvin walked to my cage and sat inside it for a while, staring at the framed photograph of me on the wall. He paid a quick visit to Chubby and Knuckles, in case either of them had come up with any bright ideas, but they hadn't.

Then, before we knew where we were, it was six o'clock.

Marvin joined his parents in the dressing-room caravan. All three of them changed into their costumes and applied their make-up. When they'd finished they sat together for a while, trying very hard to smile and look enthusiastic about the night ahead.

'Well, here we all are then!' Colin Gumbo said. 'No need for long faces! Things could be worse!'

'Could they?' Olwyn Gumbo said. 'How, exactly?'

'Well, we could . . . I mean, there could be . . . lots of worse things could happen!' Colin said.

'Like what?'

'Like . . . lots of things! Hundreds! Too many to name!'

'Name one.'

'You know, Marvin, that's what I love about your mother,' Colin sighed. 'The support she gives me. Her blind faith and unquestioning devotion.'

At six-thirty they joined the other performers and circus hands backstage. Colin Gumbo began moving slowly among them, shaking hands, wishing everybody good luck. Olwyn took the Gumbo-ettes aside for a private pep-talk, while Marvin sat with Zambini and Chubby and Knuckles – his old crew.

'Feeling in the mood tonight, big boy?' Chubby said, and gave Zambini's arm a playful squeeze.

Zambini blushed. 'I always een the mood, Chobby,' he said.

'I might have put on a couple of kilos,' Chubby told him. 'I had icecream for lunch.'

'I no drop you,' Zambini promised. 'Not eef you weigh a thousand kilos. Not unteel you burst.'

'You know, Zambini, one day your muscles are going to get so big, there won't be room left in your body for them,' Knuckles said. 'They'll start squeezing out your ears, like toothpaste.'

'Good,' Zambini replied. 'Then I no have to leesten to you.'

They laughed and joked together until seven o'clock. On the stroke of the hour, a drum roll sounded out in the ring. The crowd, which had filled the Big Top to capacity, hushed eagerly.

Colin Gumbo adjusted his top-hat and bow tie, blew a kiss to his family, then slipped through the curtain into the darkness.

'Here goes nothing,' Marvin muttered. 'We're on.'

The drum roll continued for another ten seconds. Then, to a blazing fanfare of trumpets, a spotlight cut through the blackness, and lit up Colin Gumbo in the middle of the ring.

'*Ladiiiiiiiiiiiiiiiiiiiiiiiiiiiiiiiiiiiiiiiiies and gentlemen!*' Colin Gumbo announced, bellowing as loud as he could to be heard above the sound of rapturous cheers. '*Welcome one and all, young and old, rich and poor, big and small, fat and thin, to the fantastic, the marvellous, the stupendous, the wonderful . . . NEW GUMBO CIRCUS ROYALE!*'

Cymbals clashed. Trumpets blared. The circus's

theme music began playing as the performers entered the ring for the first parade of the evening.

Marvin came first, doing flips and tumbles and somersaults, pausing every now and then to wave at the crowd.

Olwyn Gumbo came next, doing a handstand on top of a walking human pyramid formed by the Gumbo-ettes.

Then came Chubby Cupcakes, raised high on her forklift, wiggling her hips at the crowd.

Fourth was the Great Zambini. He appeared juggling ten blazing firesticks, and as he walked he flexed his muscles and twiddled his enormous black moustache.

Finally came Knuckles the Clown, riding a square-wheeled unicycle and playing the harmonica, swerving this way and that to shake hands with children in the first row.

'*What a fantastic show we have in store for you, ladies and gentlemen!*' Colin Gumbo roared, as the parade made its way slowly around the ring. '*A night of nights! A performance to end all performances! A brand-new show featuring the world's most daring and spectacular animal-free acts, in an all-juggling, all-tumbling, all-swinging, all-balancing superhuman extravaganza!*'

The crowd cheered even more wildly. Marvin

turned and caught sight of his mother, perched upside down on top of the Gumbo-ettes. He winked at her. She winked back—

Then the lights went out.

The music stopped. Colin Gumbo's microphone went dead. The Big Top was plunged into a deep and terrible darkness.

A rumbling sound filled the air, like the roar of a jumbo-jet passing overhead. The seats shook and rattled in the stands. The Gumbo-ettes lost their balance and came tumbling down onto the ring. Chubby Cupcakes almost fell from her forklift. Zambini dropped one of his blazing firesticks onto Knuckles the Clown and set fire to his hair.

'*I'm afraid there's been a mistake, ladies and gentlemen!*' a familiar voice taunted them from somewhere high above. '*The New Gumbo Circus Royale will NOT be performing this evening! The only person performing will be ME!*'

Marvin and I gazed up. The head of Dancing Dan was near the highest point of the tent, higher even than the tightrope and the high-dive platform. It looked small inside the Big Top, but it was already about the same size as a car. It continued to grow steadily as it talked.

'*If you're thinking of heading for the exits, ladies and*

gentlemen, think again!' the head said. '*They're locked! You're trapped in here, every last one of you, to witness the final and most spectacular show this miserable excuse for a circus will ever give!*'

Now the head was as big as a house, and still growing. It began to change shape in front of the audience's eyes. Its eyes became deep black caves crawling with swarms of red-bellied snakes. Its mouth became a pit of fire, belching smoke from behind bright yellow fangs. Its skin turned to scales, and something green and slimy dripped from the bite-marks on its neck.

And still it continued to grow.

To this point, the audience had sat stunned and confused. Now shouts and screams filled the air. Many hid under their seats. Those closest to the exits began a mad scramble to get out, only to find that the thick canvas flaps had been pulled down and locked shut.

All the performers were still out in the ring. They stayed loyal and defiant to the last. Even Zambini was still out there, but only because he had fainted. He lay flat on his back in the sawdust with his mouth open wide. Blazing firesticks lay strewn all around him, sputtering weakly.

As for me, I was hovering close to Marvin, ready to

do my best when Dan attacked. It wouldn't be much. In my invisible form I would be sucked up and defeated in an instant. But I had sworn an oath to defend Marvin, and I would do so till my last ghostly breath.

'You're here, aren't you, Raj?' Marvin murmured. 'Good. I'm glad. There's nobody else I'd rather be with, here at the end.'

He glanced up again at Dan's head, which was still floating at the very top of the tent, belching smoke and shooting snakes from its cavernous eyes. Judging by the grin on its face, it wasn't about to end its performance too quickly. Not while it had the ring all to itself, an audience to perform to, and a swag of helpless enemies trapped below.

'*Very brave, Gumbos, very brave!*' it said with a laugh. '*But how small and insignificant you are! No bigger than ants! Shall I crush you? Shall I fry you on the barbecue of my demon-breath? Let me count the ways I might exact my ultimate revenge!*'

'We had some great times under this Big Top, Raj,' Marvin went on. 'And we put on some pretty good shows, didn't we? Zambini and his horses. Mum and her blindfolded elephants. Chubby swinging from her trapeze. And you, doing all your marvellous tricks, standing on top of your—'

He stopped. He made a small choking noise.

At first I thought he'd swallowed something, but that wasn't it at all. He'd simply been hit by an idea so brilliant and unexpected that he'd stopped talking.

'Your box!' he whispered. 'Your red box, Raj! That's it! That's what's missing! We threw it in the bins with all the other animal equipment, and the very next day you stopped appearing!'

He didn't wait for me to answer. He sprinted to where Zambini lay sprawled in the sawdust, and began shaking him as hard as he could.

'*Zambini! Zambini, wake up! I need you to carry something for me!*'

Zambini opened one eye, saw the gigantic head of Dancing Dan rumbling and thundering above him, and fainted again.

Meanwhile, my mind was racing. Could the red box really be the answer? It was certainly the thing that I had loved most in the whole world. I was horrified to learn that it had been thrown out into the bins. But that alone wasn't enough to keep me trapped in my invisible form. Only if my home disappeared or was destroyed would I lose my power to appear. That was the ancient and unbreakable rule. And my home, my beautiful old elephant cage, was exactly where it had always been, outside near the caravans . . .

Or was it?

It hit me in a blinding flash. My cage wasn't my home! I ate and slept there, yes, but I was a performer, and my real home was here, in the ring! My beautiful red box, the site of all my greatest triumphs, was my real home after all, and it had been thrown out into the garbage! That was why I couldn't appear!

You're brilliant, Marvin! I thought. *You're not even a ghost and you figured it out! But hurry! There's not much time!*

Marvin was still shaking Zambini as hard as he could, slapping at his head and shoulders, trying to get him to move.

'Zambini! Zambini, please, you've got to help us! You're the only one who can lift it!'

Zambini rolled onto his knees and hid his head under his arms. 'Go away!' he moaned. 'Ees over! *Finito!* Everybody die!'

To my great surprise, Marvin let Zambini go. 'Fine, then,' he said. 'Forget it. You're not strong enough anyway.'

Zambini peeped out from under his arms. 'What you mean I not strong enough?' he said. 'For what?'

'Don't worry. It's way too heavy for you. You'd never lift it in a million years.'

'What you mean I no leeft it?' Zambini leapt to his feet. 'I leeft anything! Look at these moscles! You ever see moscles like thees?'

Marvin glanced up at the head of Dancing Dan, which was still showing off to the audience. Giant red-and-black snakes were now writhing through its hair. Its flaming breath had scorched sections of the canvas at the top of the tent, and set some of the smaller guyropes on fire.

'*I call this my Medusa Look,*' Dan said. '*Although the breath is more Smaug the Dragon, don't you think? I can do hags, hellcats, demons, dervishes, gargoyles, minotaurs, five- and ten-headed dogs. There's simply no end to my talent. And it sure beats getting dumb old lions to jump through hoops.*'

'Zambini and I are going to make a break for it,' Marvin called to his parents. 'We'll be back soon. No time to explain.'

'Where we going?' Zambini asked, as he ran with Marvin through the curtains into the backstage area.

'Out to get Rajah's red box,' Marvin said. 'But first we have to get through the door.'

'Why you want Rajah's box?' Zambini panted. 'We no have Rajah.'

'We will have in a minute,' Marvin said. 'That's

the whole point. Here's the exit – the flap's been padlocked. Can you break the lock?'

'I no care about lock,' Zambini said, and punched a bread-loaf-sized fist straight through the thick canvas. He tore a hole big enough for himself to get through, then he and Marvin sprinted for the industrial bins on the edge of the compound.

A minute later they were running in the opposite direction. Zambini was holding my red box high above his head. I can't describe the delight I felt when I saw that box returning to the ring. It was as if something that had been missing all my life – and most of my death – had suddenly returned.

It was showtime.

'Hurry, hurry!' Marvin puffed. 'Even Dan won't keep showing off forever!'

'You want to bet?' Zambini shoved the box in through the hole he had made in the canvas.

We were back inside.

It was like an oven inside the Big Top now. A swirling haze of smoke hung over everything. A bitter gaseous smell burned the air. The head of Dancing Dan had swelled to the size of a hot-air balloon. It was almost as big as the tent itself, and it was terrifying to look upon. With a deep, sonorous rumble, and a flash of snakes from its eyes, it stopped tormenting the audience and turned slowly to face Zambini and Marvin, fixing them in a laser-like gaze.

'*Marvin Gumbo*,' it thundered, in a voice like an avalanche of rocks. '*I have toyed with you and your family of useless circus freaks for long enough. It is time for you to meet your doom.*'

Marvin signalled to Zambini, who tossed my red box onto the sawdust in the middle of the ring. At once I felt a surge of power so strong I could barely control it. Energy exploded from everywhere inside me, shooting out like blazing comets in all directions. I concentrated my thoughts on the box in the centre of the ring, and swooped down.

'*A red box!*' Dancing Dan laughed hollowly. '*How frightening! Would you like me to stand on it for you, and do a twirl?*'

'No, that's someone else's trick,' Marvin said. With a dizzying flash of light, I appeared.

The grin on Dancing Dan's face vanished.

'*You!*' he howled. '*How did you get here? Haven't you found the elephants' graveyard yet?*'

'*I was just on my way,*' I replied. '*But I couldn't leave without saying goodbye.*'

I stood on my hind legs, and raising my trunk as high as I could, I began to suck. I sucked with more power than any vacuum cleaner that had ever been invented. I sucked with the power of a black hole devouring a star.

Immediately Dancing Dan fought back, and tried to devour me in turn.

The noise of our battle was deafening. The light we gave off was too bright to look upon. Everyone inside the Big Top fell to the ground with their eyes shut tight and their hands clasped over their ears.

'Is he winning?' Colin Gumbo shouted. 'Marvin! Is Rajah winning?'

'How should I know?' Marvin shouted back. 'I'm blind as a bat!'

'Of course he's winning!' Chubby Cupcakes shouted above the din. 'This is Rajah we're talking about! Go, Rajah, go!'

For a long time it was hard to tell which was louder: the sucking or the rumbling. Dan and I were locked in a titanic supernatural armwrestle. Neither of us could get the upper hand. Energy flowed back and forth between us like a tide. Sometimes I got bigger, sometimes he did. Sometimes I got brighter, sometimes I dimmed. But gradually the sound of sucking began to eclipse the noise of rumbling. Dan faded away to almost nothing. His neck stretched out into a long, wispy 'V' shape, and he slowly began disappearing up my trunk.

'*I've got you now!*' I said triumphantly. '*I've pulled the plug on you! Soon there'll be nothing left of you but a bad smell!*'

'*It's not over yet . . . hose-nose . . .*' Dan growled, but even as he said it he knew it was. His eyes were rolling. His face was stretched and elongated, like a reflection in a trick mirror. Already his chin had disappeared, along with his lower jaw and both his earlobes.

He was unravelling in front of my eyes like a badly knitted sweater.

'Do it, Rajah!' I heard Marvin yell. He was jumping up and down, shaking both fists in the air. 'Sock it to 'im, baby!'

'Holy melted mozzarella!' Zambini said. 'He slurping Dan up like a meelk-a-shake!'

Soon only Dancing Dan's forehead remained. The smoke and heat inside the Big Top had vanished. The fires on the guyropes had gone out. The audience had got up from behind their seats, or wherever they'd been hiding, and were gazing in confusion at the strange spectacle unfolding before their eyes.

Some were leafing through their program notes, trying to find the part that explained about the elephant and the giant head.

'*I'm fading* . . .' Dan whispered, his voice no more than a faint hiss drifting across the ring. '*I can feel it. Everything's . . . draining away . . .*'

'Show's over, Dan,' Marvin said. 'Time to take your final bow. I'm sure they'll have your champagne and your red carpet ready, down in Hell.'

'*No! I can't let it . . . end like this!*' Dan made one final effort to shake himself free. '*Slurped up in my prime! Sucked into an elephant's nostril! Please! Not into the trunk! Anything but that!*'

Fwwp!

I sucked up the last remaining hair on Dancing Dan's head.

He was gone.

There was a silence. The lights came back on. The music started up, exactly where it had left off. Colin Gumbo tapped his radio microphone, and found it was working as well as ever.

'*Ladiiiiiiiiiies and gentlemen!*' he announced. '*Welcome back, one and all, after that long and extremely rude interruption! As you may have guessed, that was the ghost of Dancing Dan, getting extremely big-headed and trying to take over the show! And he might have succeeded, if it weren't for one very gutsy ghost elephant, who very nearly didn't make it here tonight! Please put your hands together and thank the King of the Jungle, the*

Prince of Pachyderms, the greatest circus elephant the world has ever known . . . **RAJAH-H-H-H-H-H!!!**'

A cheer went up that was so loud it was heard by men on a fishing trawler sixteen kilometres out to sea. The spotlight fell on me in the middle of the ring. I flapped my ears, twirled once on my red box, then trumpeted as loud as I could. Marvin ran to my side and I curled my trunk tightly around him.

'Don't go yet, Raj!' Marvin said. 'This is our big night!'

I was already beginning to fade. I knew I wouldn't have long. But sometimes even dead elephants can get time off.

I hoisted Marvin up and held him high above my head as the cheers continued. Then I set him down on my shoulders, and the two of us began a slow lap of honour around the ring.

This was one show I wasn't going to miss for the world.